I0523007

BACK HOME TO YOU

MAGGIE WILD

Back Home to You is a work of fiction. Names, characters, places, and incidents are a product of the author's imagination. Locales and public names are sometimes used for atmospheric purposes. Any similarities to actual people, living or dead, or to businesses, companies, events, institutions, or locales is completely coincidental.

Copyright © 2021 by Maggie Wild

All rights reserved. No part of this publication may be reproduced, distributed or transmitted in any form or by any means, including photocopying, recording, video, or other electronic or mechanical methods, without prior written permission of the publisher, except in the cases of brief quotations embodied in critical reviews and certain other noncommercial uses permitted by copyright law.

Published by Steel Rose Press, Santa Rosa, California

Publication Date: June 2021

ISBN: 978-0-9986969-7-3 (ebook)

ISBN: 978-0-9986969-9-7 (paperback)

Cover art by Book Cover Zone

For my mum
Always close, no matter how far away

CHAPTER ONE

HARRIET "HARRY" Belmont was halfway across the Atlantic when she realized her remarkable life was, in fact, one great, giant flop. As the flight attendant handed her a third glass of champagne (or was it a fourth?) and she replayed her *Deep Sleep in Twenty Minutes* meditation app —also for the third (or was it the fourth?) time—an image flashed through her mind. A deck of playing cards built into an elaborate pyramid, the Queen of Hearts pulled out, and the whole thing tumbling down.

It sounded so dramatic, even to Harry, but actually, it was true.

It had all started with her job, the three p.m. summons to Human Resources. Harry had seen enough chagrined employees shuffling through the glass lobby of Visionere's San Francisco headquarters on a Friday afternoon, their careers packed into a single cardboard box, to know that this meeting wasn't to deliver good news. Harry eyed her cactus, Spike, the photo of herself hiking the Inca Trail back when she took actual time off between contracts, and the red stoneware mug she'd bought on a getaway weekend at the coast with Tom.

"I think we might be on the move again, Spike," she said. The cactus said nothing, as usual.

"Re-org," is what she'd expected Judith, the HR Director, to say. Or "contract renegotiations"—something buzzy and non-specific to let Harry know it was time to move on. No biggie. She'd been there before and always landed on her feet. But Harry was in for a surprise.

"We've received a complaint," Judith said, doing everything in her power to keep her mascara-fringed eyes locked on Harry's file.

"About me?"

"It was brought to us by another employ-*ee*."

Harry hated the way Judith pronounced employee, dragging out the last syllable as if persons in employment were a disdainful inconvenience.

"A complaint about what?" Harry asked as she ran through the details of her current project. Deliverables were delivered, problems solved, deadlines met, all on schedule and under budget. She'd earned a reputation in the tech world for working this way on every project since the start of her career, which is why her employers always offered to renew her contracts. She usually declined, never staying in any job or any city for longer than two years. But this time she'd hoped to stick around.

"The employ-*ee* in question reported an 'inter-employ-*ee* relationship' that they considered inappropriate." Judith even provided the air quotes. The woman was a walking cliche.

Still, "inter-employee relationship" made Harry flinch. She meant Tom.

Harry had known from the start that a relationship with

her senior team leader would be frowned upon if they were ever found out, so for six months they'd been extra discreet. They were never more than civil to one another at work, never went for drinks or lunch near the office, never even sat close to one another when co-workers were around. They'd sometimes venture out to an exclusive restaurant, and once to the ballet, but most of their relationship was conducted behind closed doors at Harry's apartment, or at small romantic B&Bs along the California coast. Harry allowed herself a smile at the memory of their most recent escape: two nights in a cottage overlooking the rugged Mendocino coastline, a breakfast of homemade coffee cakes and savories delivered to their door each morning. Long walks around the headland, hand-in-hand as they watched for whale spouts out to sea. Delicious dinners over which they talked about places they both wanted to visit. And long languid afternoons making love in the high four-poster bed, her skin pressed into crisp white sheets, and Tom transporting her from a fluffy cloud of bedding to a fluffy cloud of nirvana.

They knew the consequences of being seen together, so they were always careful. The odds of running into someone from work were lower than the odds of spotting Bigfoot.

Harry pursed her lips, the vision of Tom's body vanishing in a puff. "This employ-*ee*, does he—or she—have evidence of said alleged relationship?"

Judith straightened. "She—or he—didn't name names." Except mine, thought Harry. "But this person felt strongly that such a relationship was taking place and that, if such a relationship were to happen, it might jeopardize the team and the project. You understand, of course, that we must take this kind of issue very seriously."

Harry understood perfectly. She and Tom had talked

about the company policy and what they'd do if they were found out. It wouldn't do to allow a relationship between a senior executive and an underling, so one of them would have to go. Tom had seniority and an impeccable record; Harry was a contractor. She was the disposable asset, so of course she had to go.

If losing her contract renewal option was the worst news Judith had delivered, Harry could have coped. She had highly sought-after, transferable skills, and an excellent track record. But that hadn't been the end. As Judith finished up going through the terms of Harry's termination and handed Harry an envelope containing her final paycheck, she'd dropped her professional demeanor for a moment.

"I'm sorry to see you go, Harry," she said. "We'll miss you around here."

"It's been a good ride," Harry said begrudgingly, then immediately regretted her choice of words.

"Tom especially will be sorry to lose you from the team."

Harry's head snapped up, scanning Judith's face to see if this was an off-hand comment or if the whistle-blower had, in fact, named names.

"You'll be hard to replace," Judith said, turning away from Harry to stack papers on her credenza, tapping them into a perfect block. "But I've promised Tom I'll look for your replacement while he and Meredith are in the Caymans."

Harry's heart stopped. "Meredith? His ex-wife?"

"Ex? Oh, no," said Judith. "Tom and Meredith aren't divorced. Given that you worked under him, surely you knew that."

But Harry had not known that. From her first day at

Visionere, the office rumor mill had made it clear that Tom and Meredith's marriage had been on the rocks for years. Meredith never came to any spouses-included work events. In fact, it was after the company holiday party that Harry and Tom had first hit it off. Harry made discreet enquiries at the office about Tom's availability. The consensus was that he and Meredith were no longer together. She even asked Tom about his ex-wife once it was clear they were going to be more than colleagues. "Ancient history," is what he'd said, and she had no cause to doubt him.

Less than an hour after Judith dropped her bombshell, Harry jockeyed her meager possessions into the back seat of an Uber and called Tom. Judith had it wrong about him being in the Caymans. He was in Florida, touring manufacturers, or so he'd said. When her call went to voicemail, she told herself he was probably out to dinner, entertaining clients. Definitely not lounging by the pool with his wife.

She texted. "Got fired. Need to talk."

Nothing.

Frustrated, she broke their cardinal rule and called his personal cell.

After the third ring, his deep, warm voice oozed through the airwaves, the sound of conversation and quiet music in the background. He was at a restaurant, just as she'd imagined. "Tom Steele speaking."

"It's me. I need to talk to you."

His voice turned icy so fast, as if the San Francisco fog had rolled in on a warm October day. "I'm in the middle of something at the moment. Can I call you later?"

"I got fired," Harry said.

"I heard. I'll take care of it, I promise, but I can't talk right now."

"Then perhaps I could talk to your wife." Harry hated

her shrewish outburst. That's not how she wanted to behave. She was a reasonable person. She would listen to Tom, get his side of the story, talk through the situation like civilized adults. No reasonable solution, she believed, came from making threats.

Tom said nothing at first, but she heard a muffled voice —a woman's—and the rustle of clothes as Tom moved. As the noise of conversation faded, she could hear the background music more clearly. Calypso music if she wasn't mistaken.

"Harry, darling. I'm so sorry about the contract. I've already put out feelers for you. You'll be snapped up in no time."

Harry flinched from a sharp stab under her ribs, somewhere between her gut and her heart. "You knew this was coming, and you didn't tell me?"

"I know. I..."

"You knew, and you left the country?"

"I..."

"With your wife." It wasn't a question anymore. She had all the answers she needed.

Tom blew out a stress sigh and she could picture him running a hand through his wavy hair, the light catching the first salt and pepper flecks, his shirt riding up to expose olive skin above the belt of his jeans, the ripple of the taut abs he worked so hard to maintain. Whenever he made that move, she could never resist slipping her hand into the gap, savoring the warmth of his skin, pulling him towards her. He never resisted. Now she wondered if she was alone in her desire for that enticing patch of skin. Or did it drive his wife crazy, too?

"Is it true?" Harry asked, just to be certain.

"It's complicated, Harry."

"Not really. Either you lied about being divorced or you didn't."

"I never said Merrie and I were divorced."

The sound of her name in his voice cut into Harry. *Merrie*, a pet name, not *Meredith*, not *my ex*. And now that Harry thought about it, she knew it was true. "Ancient history" could mean a lot of things, including a long and possibly happy marriage. Harry had chosen an explanation that suited her needs. She wanted Tom to be divorced, and she had made it so.

"Look, Harry," said Tom. "I'm taking some time off until the dust settles. Let's talk when I get back. I'll make this right with you, I promise."

"I won't be here," Harry said, because suddenly her heart no longer wanted to talk about Tom's wife, no longer wanted to think about the stack of deceits piling up at her feet. Her heart didn't want to look at their clandestine weekend getaways in this harsh new light, didn't want to re-examine their secret romance, their discretion no longer a tactic to preserve their jobs, but a way for a cheating husband to avoid getting caught.

"Harry, come on," Tom said. "I screwed up. I'm sorry. But think about it. Now we're not working together, we're free."

"No," Harry said. "*I'm* free. You still have a job and a wife."

As she hung up on Tom, she made a silent vow: Never again would she mix business and pleasure.

On her first unemployed Monday after Tom's betrayal—because let's face it, there was no other way to describe his lies and utter disregard for her—Harry sat at the breakfast bar in her tiny kitchen watching the rising sun turn the windows of the neighboring towers golden, and scanning recruitment websites for job opportunities. She wasn't afraid of a fresh start. Working on contract suited her, shaking things up every couple of years. She'd moved so many times, she'd bought a special carrying case for Spike. Two years in Atlanta, where she'd first found Spike at a farmer's market, then two in San Diego. A stint in Austin, Spike's favorite climate, and then to San Francisco, where Spike had surprised her with his first flower.

"What do you think about the East Coast, Spike?"

The cactus didn't answer, and she wondered if he had grown to love The City by the Bay, too. Maybe they'd both been thinking of putting down roots here.

"New York," Harry said. "Or maybe Boston. Just you and me, Spike." She blinked at a drop of moisture forming on the rim of her eye. "Just you and me."

When her phone rang, she was surprised to see her mother's name on the screen. For a brief moment, Harry wondered if her mother had sensed her only daughter's need for comfort and compassion. Then Harry remembered that her mother was Barbara.

"I thought you and Graham were in Portugal?" Harry said. "Is everything okay?"

"We are in Portugal and everything's fine," Barbara said. "We're having a glorious time. And then your grandmother got a letter from the hospital. About her hip."

Harry closed the lid of her laptop. Her gran had been suffering with her hip for years, gradually slowing down from her usual breakneck speed of living, the walkable area of her world shrinking along with it. Despite Barbara's insistence that her mother seek private health care and even offering to pay, Harry's gran insisted on waiting for the NHS to come through with a hip replacement operation. And now they had.

"She's going in a week from today," Barbara said. "Typical inconvenient timing. Graham and I will be cruising in the Med until the following Friday, and who knows if I'll have cell service? If you have time, I was thinking you might ring her while she's in the hospital. Keep her chin up a bit."

"Of course. Are you going up to stay with her after?"

"Stay with her?"

"When you get back? I imagine she'll need help for a couple of weeks until she can get around on her own."

"I can't. You know that, Harry."

Harry did know. Her childhood was a combination of living with Barbara, living with Barbara and her boyfriend *du jour*, and living with Barbara and Tony, Harry's first stepfather before Graham. She'd never known her real father—was never certain if her mother did either—and Tony left when Harry was fourteen. After that, the three generations of Belmont women lived together for almost a year. Barbara drove Gran around the bend, and even Harry was relieved when her mother met Graham and announced another move. Harry had drawn the line there. She was tired of chasing after her mother as her mother chased after another man. She opted to stay with Gran, Barbara had barely objected, and the following three years had been among the most content of Harry's life.

"I'll go and stay with her," Harry blurted without thinking.

"Oh, you don't have to do that. You're busy."

Harry decided not to explain that "busy" was the last thing she was. She could spend some time with Gran, get serious about her job search while Gran was in the hospital, and stay long enough to get Gran back on her feet. "Actually, now's the perfect time. I could do it."

"But what about your work? And your life. You can't just drop everything for me."

Harry didn't bother pointing out that she was dropping everything for Gran. The center of Barbara's universe had always been Barbara, and Harry had long ago given up wishing it was any other way. And as for dropping everything? Harry looked around her apartment. She'd always enjoyed the minimalist decor and the simplicity of the home she'd created. But, except for Spike, it could have been a hotel room. It felt like a temporary place created by someone waiting to set up a proper home. And as for dropping her life? Her life had already dropped *her*.

"I'm coming," she told her mother. "And that's final."

She bought a plane ticket with her stack of unused miles, and when her roommate, Taz, who worked nights as a bartender, emerged from her room, Harry announced her plans. Taz agreed to take responsibility for Spike's care, promising not to over-water him, and asked if her sister could stay while Harry was away.

"I'll be back before you know it, Spike," Harry said. Her recent sour lemons were turning into lemonade, after all.

TWO DAYS LATER, as her plane bounced through a thick layer of cloud, Harry felt like she was truly making a clean break.

"Good morning from the flight deck." The captain's voice came over the plane's PA system. "We hope you had a pleasant night's sleep."

Harry stretched her neck, feeling a knot at her shoulder. She wasn't sure if it was a flight-related crick or stress.

"We'll be starting our descent into Manchester shortly.

The weather on the ground is partly cloudy with a slight chance of afternoon drizzle."

Harry peered through the tiny oval window at the landscape below. The vast ocean butted up against the crenelated coastline of the British Isles and gave way to a swath of green—rolling hills and patchwork fields—dotted with tiny villages.

Her seat mate yawned and peeled back a black sleep mask, rubbing under his eyes as if he'd just woken from the deepest sleep. "Good to be home," he said.

"Yes," said Harry, politely.

"Are you going home or visiting?"

Harry hesitated, unsure how to answer what ought to be a simple question. "I'm from here originally, but I live in San Francisco now."

"Lucky you," he said. "Still, there's no place like home, is there?"

Harry smiled, but she wasn't entirely sure she agreed. "Home" was a complicated concept. She'd called San Francisco home for close to three years now. And yet, whenever she talked about England and the village where she'd grown up, she always referred to it as home.

But Hope had not been home to Harry for a long time. She'd left for university at eighteen, and hadn't been back, except for brief visits, since landing the job in Atlanta after graduation. Nor did she ever plan to. Some people say you can't go home again, and Harry firmly believed that was true. As soon as this trip was over, Harry would go back to the States, where she belonged.

"No," Harry said. "There's no place like home."

The drive from Manchester Airport to the little village of Hope took exactly an hour, and the taxi driver did not stop talking the entire way.

"How long you home for?" he asked as he tossed her Tumi suitcase into the trunk—or rather the boot—of his taxi and opened the door for Harry.

"Three weeks," Harry said.

"Must be nice," the driver said. "Are you a school-teacher?"

Harry frowned, scanning her appearance for the clue the driver had picked up to decide she worked in education. "Um, no?"

"Oh, I just assumed with you being able to take all that time off, you must be a teacher or something."

Harry bristled at the reminder of her extended break. "I'm in tech." And she left it at that, hoping the brief expla-nation would stop the driver from asking more questions. It didn't.

"You're a good granddaughter," he said, when he pried out of Harry that she was staying with her gran. And then he launched into a story about his wife's gallbladder and how his one son never even came to see her.

Harry kept her brain sufficiently engaged to make all the right noises in all the right places, but as the driver navi-gated the twisty hilltop roads, and the scenery zipped by, she wondered if she had been a good granddaughter. The wave of relief she'd felt at being free to help her gran had surprised her, but it didn't diminish the guilt she carried for having moved so far away.

As the "Welcome to Hope Valley" sign came into view, Harry had the strange sensation of plummeting down a deep hole only to land right back where she'd started. Instead of returning as the success story she'd once envi-sioned, she was going home fired, dumped, and missed only by an intimacy-averse plant. She imagined old friends and neighbors asking about her life, and the answers she'd be obligated to give.

"Make a left here," she shouted to the taxi driver.

He glanced at her in the mirror, then screeched the car down the narrow one-lane road of High Riding Lane. A hundred yards down, the trees thinned to reveal a small half-moon parking spot on the right. When Harry asked the driver to pull over, he shrugged as if her request was far from the strangest he'd ever had.

Harry hauled her jet-lagged body from the car, her joints stiff from the hours of inactivity, her vision bleary from being awake when her body thought it should be asleep. She staggered to the edge of the overlook, her breath catching in her chest. In the valley below, the village where she'd spent her teen years nestled, the church spire marking the spot like a flag in a sandcastle. She'd been safe and happy in Hope, but she couldn't forget the shame that radiated from her mother when they were left with no option but to move in with Gran. When Harry left Hope to go to university two hundred miles away, she swore she would never be like Barbara and make a big enough mess of her life that she'd have to come home. And now, here she was.

"It's only temporary," she reminded herself. "Everything is temporary." She was here for a visit, to help Gran, to be a good granddaughter, as the taxi driver said. And then she'd go home.

She breathed, the knot in her chest releasing. As she stretched and looked around the turnout, her gaze fell on a wooden gate in the stone wall. She stepped through it and down a few rough steps to a wooden plank bench hidden from the road. Nostalgia washed over her, a memory of hours spent in this spot slowly coming into focus. She used to come up here with Jamie. *Jamie Forrest*! Harry laughed to herself, a long-forgotten feeling of excitement stirring inside her. Jamie would drive them up here in his dad's old Ford and they'd make out until their faces were raw. They'd sit on this very bench in the summer twilight and talk about their plans for the future. How she would forge a career in a cutting-edge technology, how Jamie would open a restaurant in London and be a world-renowned chef.

They'd kept their promises, too. They'd both followed their ambitions, made grand plans, and seen them through. Gran had sent Harry a clipping from the local paper years ago. Jamie and his business partner in their swanky Soho eatery—Stone, or Brick, or some hip one-word name. She'd been so pleased for him, with just the slightest pang of wistfulness that she hadn't been there to see it. But Harry had made it, too. She hadn't exactly changed the world, but she'd worked for a string of tech start-ups and, in her own way, made an impact. She and Jamie had gone their separate ways, forging the lives they'd planned, just not with one another.

Something caught in her throat, a raw emotion. A lump of reality choking her breath. Truth was, nothing about her so-called success was substantial. Her whole way of life was tenuous. And the fact that she could leave for almost a month and no one would miss her made her realize how alone she really was.

A small sob escaped from her throat.

Pull it together, Harry.

She would not cry about this, and she especially would not cry about this to her gran. The big mess with Tom was just a glitch, a huge mistake to get so attached, but survivable. She would use her time away to get her life back on track. Get in, take care of Gran, find a job, go home. Three weeks and she'd be back in the saddle.

"Forget Tom," she told herself. It was time to move on. She could use her own contacts to find a new job. She could look for work online from here as easily as from San Francisco, attend interviews via video. And wouldn't it be nice to spend some quality time with Gran, catch up on some sleep, take in some fresh country air, and regroup? A working holiday of sorts.

She climbed back into the taxi and asked the driver to head for Hope.

"I can always find hope," he said, and chuckled to himself.

Harry laughed too, finally heartened that everything would work out fine. But as they reached the junction of High Riding Lane, a white van zipped around the turn and shot down the lane. Harry caught only the briefest glimpse of the driver—a flash of cropped chestnut hair, a cheeky smile, a mouth she'd kissed a thousand times.

Jamie Forrest wasn't in London after all. He was right here in Hope. And now she'd have to hear all about his success when her life was in utter shambles.

CHAPTER TWO

JAMIE FORREST narrowly missed the taxi as he swung his van into High Riding Lane. As he threw the driver an apologetic smile, he glimpsed the woman in the back seat. *American,* he thought. You could always spot American tourists on the rare occasions they passed through Hope. It wasn't any particular facial feature or way of dressing that set them apart; they had an air about them, confident in a way even the most accomplished British people never seemed to be. Alexis had been that way, always supremely confident in her ability to conquer the world. And, of course, she'd been right. Jamie, not so much.

He pulled the van into the half-moon parking spot and took out his lunch, a cheese and pickle sandwich on whole-grain bread. It was a simple lunch, but with the rich, sharp cheddar cheese from Morton's dairy, the tangy home-made pickle from Sarah's Kitchen, and the crusty bread baked fresh that morning at Hope Valley Bakery, this sandwich was as big a treat as any gourmet feast.

Jamie had always loved food. His mother had embarrassed him as a boy by telling people that, when most toddlers reached the stage of picking peas and carrots from a plastic tray, Jamie was already eating whatever the rest of the family ate. At two years old, he'd shocked the landlady of a bed-and-breakfast by eating a full English at the table. As a teenager, he had big dreams of becoming a chef, opening a hot restaurant in the heart of London. He'd done it, too. And then he'd been burned—not physically, thankfully, but he'd been scarred all the same. Two years later he was back in Hope, determined to start again. He'd found his calling after all, and in many ways his life was even better than the one he'd once imagined.

As the creator of Local Goodness, a meal kit delivery service using only locally-sourced ingredients, he got to support local farmers, small producers—like his friends Michael and Sarah—and culinary artisans in the region. Using their products, he'd experimented in his own kitchen, and developed menus of seasonal recipes. He created customized meal kits for one to six people, delivered in reusable boxes to customers in the many villages surrounding Hope. His suppliers gained new business, his customers valued the low carbon footprint of supporting local producers, and Jamie loved... well, Jamie loved it all. He loved meeting with producers to sample their products; he loved taking those products back to his kitchen and experimenting with recipes; and most of all, he loved delivering the kits and chatting with his customers about the contents of their boxes. Jamie loved talking about food. The trouble was, Local Goodness was such a hit that talking about food was all he did these days. He had a part-time assistant to handle the orders, but needed to hire more help, just to keep up with demand. And if he ever wanted to get back in the kitchen, he'd have to find employees he could trust to manage the whole operation. That was easier said than done.

He pushed the whole idea aside and took another bite of his sandwich. Perhaps he could recreate this flavor combination in some kind of tart, or maybe a cheese-and-pickle Wellington. Maybe tonight he could put off paperwork and just cook. He put down the sandwich, his appetite gone. If he put off the admin, he'd be even further behind tomorrow. May as well get back to work now.

He pulled up the list of his afternoon deliveries. Only five more stops today, a shorter-than-usual day. Someone must have cancelled. As he checked the list, he spotted a mistake. He gritted his teeth and called Ollie, trying to keep his nerves calm. He counted nine rings before anyone answered.

"Local Goodness, Oliver speaking. How may I help you?"

"Nine rings, Ollie. What took you so long?"

"Sorry, Bossman. I've been looking at this route-mapping app again, and honestly, I don't think it's efficient. If we—"

"Ollie," Jamie said. "No amount of efficient routing will help us if we don't keep our customers happy, and we can't do that if you won't answer the phone."

"Sorry, Bossman. What's up?"

Jamie curled his lips in and bit down hard, half furious, half laughing at Ollie. The kid was... different. He had brains, no doubt about it, but they didn't seem to work like other people's brains. He was creative, always on stage for every Hope Valley Players production, and analytical too. That combination caused him to solve problems in a round-about way. Take Jamie's delivery routes. He had always looked at his daily stops and picked what he'd thought was the most efficient route from Point A to Point D, via Points B and C. Then Jamie's mother had asked a favor for a friend from her Ladies Group, and Jamie had agreed to hire Ollie. He'd taken one look at Jamie's routes and shaken his head. He'd devised a system that seemed to head straight for Point Z and work backwards through the whole alphabet. It made no sense to Jamie, but when he tried it, he discovered he was back at the office faster than ever before. It should have left him with more time to play in his kitchen, but Local Goodness kept growing and Jamie couldn't keep up.

From a business point of view, success wasn't the worst problem to have, but things had been going wrong. Last week, he'd messed up a special order from a long-time customer. Yesterday, he'd somehow got two orders switched so that a customer with a nut allergy got Pad Thai and Trout Almandine. Jamie was rushing, and if he didn't slow down, he'd lose the trust of the customers he'd worked so hard to gain. Or worse, accidentally kill them!

"Ollie, can you double-check the order for Mrs. Belmont? I think it got duplicated."

"Nope," Ollie said. "It's right."

Jamie frowned. "Well, could you at least check?"

"No need, Bossman. I took the order myself. She said her daughter's coming to stay, and she's hopeless in the kitchen, so she needs a double order for the next three days, then back to her usual after that."

"You're sure," Jamie said. Old Mrs. Belmont never complained about her daughter, but Jamie knew that Barbara Belmont-Sissons visited her mother about every other blue moon and stayed only an hour. It was possible she might stay to help Mrs. Belmont before her hip operation, but Jamie doubted it. Barbara was more likely to hire help than do it herself.

For a brief moment, Jamie's mind flitted to Barbara's only daughter. Harry Belmont. Now there was a blast from the past. He hadn't seen Harry in years. He stared at the view ahead of him, a goofy smile forming on his lips as he thought about the two most blissful summers of his teenaged life—the summers he'd learned everything he needed to know about love in the capable hands of Harry Belmont. How many hours had they spent in this exact spot, Harry igniting Jamie's teenage desires? Harry had lit a fire under his career dreams, too, convincing him to go to culinary school, making him believe he could succeed.

And then she'd broken his tender teenage heart.

"Bossman?" Ollie said, as a glob of pickle slipped from the sandwich into Jamie's lap. "Are you still eating your lunch?"

"Trying," said Jamie, staring at the chunk of carrot and spicy sauce now seeping into the fabric of his jeans.

"Only it's 1:21 and you're officially behind schedule. If you want to get done and back to the office before the school run starts, you'd better get a move on."

Jamie sighed. Wasn't he supposed to be the boss? In charge of his own time? Wasn't that a benefit of being self-employed? He appreciated Ollie being a stickler for time and keeping him on track, but if he didn't even have time to eat a quick sandwich, something wasn't right. He glanced at the folder of job applications in the passenger seat. That was it. He was going to go through them tonight and set up some interviews. If he didn't change something soon, his business was going to implode.

"Aye-aye, Cap'n," Jamie said, tossing the sandwich back into its bag. He took one last glimpse of his favorite view in the world and pointed the van back to the main road.

At his next stop, he helped his customer with a stuck

lid on a jar, and gave another an opinion on new tile for her kitchen. He spent way too long admiring photographs of a longtime client's new granddaughter and threw a stick for another customer's dog so many times his arm ached. When he arrived at Hilltop Farm, home of his long-time customers, Callum and Jess, Jamie was already behind schedule. He crunched up the driveway, rehearsing his apologies, and rang the doorbell, setting off a chorus of greetings from the trio of beagles. The door opened, and the dogs squeezed out, winding around Jamie's legs as if he was the very person they'd waited their whole lives to see.

"Leave Uncle Jamie alone, girls," Callum said to the dogs, who paid not the slightest attention. "Obviously, I'm just as excited to see you," he said to Jamie.

"Appreciate you keeping it subdued," said Jamie, handing Callum the box. "How's the project coming?"

Callum pushed his black-framed glasses up on this head and rubbed his eyes. "Slow. Client's a nightmare, to be honest, but I think we're making progress. Time for a coffee?"

Callum and Jess were architects, running their business from home. They often asked Jamie in for coffee. He had the feeling they didn't see too many other people during the day, and they enjoyed his company. Jamie was tempted to accept the offer, but Ollie would not be pleased if he stopped today. Nor would his remaining customers.

Jamie shook his head. "Wish I could, but I'm on a tight schedule today." When Callum looked disappointed, he added, "Maybe next time?" Jamie hated not delivering his full level of customer service. He had to hire that help sooner rather than later.

By the time Jamie passed the village school, traffic was

already at a crawl. He was more than an hour behind schedule when he arrived at Mrs. Belmont's.

Like most people in the village, Mrs. Belmont left her back door unlocked and had instructed Jamie to let himself in with deliveries. Balancing the two boxes on one arm, he rapped twice on the door and pushed it open, calling out as he stepped inside. "Just me, Mrs. B. I'll put it on the table."

He waited for the old lady to respond, an additional perk he offered with his delivery service, checking in to make sure his more elderly customers were okay. Voices chattered in the front room. She was fine; she just hadn't heard him. "Delivery's here, Mrs. B," he called, louder. "Do you want me to put your perishables away?"

"I'll do it," said a voice from the kitchen door. And there stood Harry Belmont.

Something in the bottom of his belly danced itself into a knot. Not Mrs. B's daughter; her *grand*daughter. Trust Ollie to get it wrong about Barbara coming to stay. "I thought you were your mother," was all he could say.

Harry laughed. "Please tell me that was supposed to be a compliment."

"It was," he stammered. "Ollie said your mother was... and I just... Wow," he said at last. "You look great."

She hadn't changed a bit, and yet she looked a world away from the teenage girl he'd known. This new Harry had a mature air of confidence about her, pulled together and in control. She wore an expensive-looking cashmere sweater that grazed over her neat body, her still-slender hips wrapped in perfectly-fitting jeans. But then her smooth tanned face broke into that wide toothy smile and she was once again the Harry he knew.

"Jamie?" she said, her high cheekbones almost glowing with joy. "Jamie Forrest?"

He held out his arms. "The same."

She pulled him into an exuberant hug. "What are you doing here?"

"I live here."

"I thought you were in London."

His smile twitched down and he forced it back up, suddenly feeling the need to defend his entire life. "I came back. Set up in business here." He indicated the boxes sitting on the table, their contents slowly inching back to room temperature. "What are you doing here?"

Did he imagine it, or did her smile falter, too?

"I came to help my gran," she said, suddenly gaining interest in the boxes.

She had a hint of an American accent now, a honey-coating to her words, as if she'd chewed them once or twice before letting them out.

"So, what's new in your world?" he asked. "You married? Kids?" Her smile dropped for a second time, and he clamped his mouth shut, too late to silence his presumptuous question.

"Too busy for a husband, and I have white carpets, so no kids for me." She laughed again, her full lips parting to reveal those teeth again. He'd always loved that mouth. But her laugh was strained. There was more to her nonchalance than she was letting on. *You still can't get anything past me, Harry Belmont.*

"You?" she asked. "Some lucky woman snap you up yet?"

Now it was his turn to force a laugh. "They keep trying. But you know me. I'm elusive." It was supposed to be a joke, but it had landed a little too close to the truth. After Harry, he'd fallen in love again. Just once. But his stupid, soppy heart got itself broken all over again, and he'd decided it was safer to give romance a wide berth. After that, he married his work and, until recently, they'd been happy together.

Harry looked away, her smile gone, a pensive look on her face now. God, she was still beautiful, more beautiful than ever, perhaps. Yes, definitely more. Her shoulder-length dark hair was straight and sleek, no wispy strands escaping. She moved with grace around the kitchen table, peeking into the boxes he'd left.

"This looks fantastic," she said, the smile popping back. "I get meal kits at home, but my gran's been raving about yours."

"Can I give you a hand putting them away?" Jamie said before he could stop himself. What was he doing? He needed to get out of here before Harry asked more questions he didn't want to answer.

But Harry pulled away. "You're kind to offer, but I'm sure I'll be fine."

She stacked the boxes on the table, building a wall of dinners between them.

"Well, I'd better get going," he said, taking the hint. "Got a few more stops to make." A lie. "Here's my card in case you need anything." He slid the card towards her and immediately wished he could pull it back.

"Thanks," she said. "Well, I'm here for a while, so I'm sure I'll see you around."

"Three days, I hear."

She frowned. "Three weeks."

Jamie stammered. "My assistant said your gran wanted a double order for three days, so I assumed..."

"She's having her op on Monday, and they'll keep her in, so I'll be eating alone. We'll double up again once she's home, if that's okay."

"Okay, right. Yes, of course. Totally misunderstood."

Jamie was babbling. *Pull it together, Forrest,* he told himself. *You're acting like a baboon.*

"So, I guess I'll be seeing you around," said Harry.

Jamie froze in place. Three weeks. Three full weeks of running into Harry Belmont. Twenty-one days of opportunity for her to ask about his career, ask what happened to his restaurant, why he didn't follow his dreams. Practically an entire month of being around the woman who broke his heart so that they could both succeed, only for him to come home a failure. "That's great," he said.

Just great.

CHAPTER THREE

THE NEXT MORNING, Harry woke up in her childhood bedroom, feeling like she'd slept for a year. Gran had stripped the red-and-white wallpaper of Harry's youth and replaced it with a soothing pale blue. She'd replaced Harry's lumpy single bed with a nice double with a firm mattress and an adjustable frame that Harry could tilt by remote control into a relaxing position. The bed had crisp pale sheets and a fluffy down quilt topped with a heavy hand-made cotton blanket that pressed Harry deep into the bed, cocooned safely under its weight. Harry stretched her body down the length of the soft bed and yawned lazily. And then she remembered Jamie Forrest. She flung back the bedding, feeling the cold morning air on her skin, and went for a hot shower.

Of all the people she might have run into on her first night back in Hope, why did it have to be Jamie? She had dumped Jamie, probably broken his teenage heart, because she was so certain they needed to be apart if they were to follow their dreams. She'd been right. Of course she'd been right. They'd been teenagers, far too young to be thinking about commitment. But now, here she was, jobless and single, with her grand plans in shreds, and the last person she wanted to see her like this was Jamie.

She turned off the shower and toweled herself dry. Find another job. That's what she had to do. She'd start looking today, in between spending time with Gran. And she'd avoid Jamie Forrest, at least until she could look him in the eye and say (truthfully) that she was taking some well-earned time off before her next big contract. He'd never need to know that her fabulous life was really a big, hot mess.

Harry found Gran in the kitchen, hobbling with a cane as she tried to make tea with one hand. "Let me," Harry said.

"You're supposed to be my guest," Gran said.

Harry looked at her from under her lowered brow. "Since when did I become a guest in my own home?" She stopped herself from saying more. This wasn't her home, hadn't been for more than a decade. She'd have to remember that.

"You look tired," Gran said, passing the teapot to Harry but hovering at her shoulder.

"Jet lag. And I've been busy."

"How's the job?"

Harry tried on a confident smile. "I'm looking for something new. I'm ready for a change."

Gran narrowed her eyes, and Harry knew she still couldn't get anything past her. How many hours had she and Gran spent talking at this table? Harry could always open up to Gran in a way she never could with her mother.

"I've done something stupid," Harry said, and told Gran about the break-up with Tom, keeping the worst details to a minimum.

"Oh, Harry," Gran said, kindly. "Why do you always go for unavailable men?"

"I don't. I…"

Gran gave Harry a familiar look, the wise yet caring one Harry knew well.

Harry sighed. "It's my fault. I stayed too long, let myself get comfortable."

"First of all, it is not your fault. That man is a disgrace to the institution of marriage. I know your granddad's eyes roved once in a while, but he didn't follow with his hands, and he certainly didn't follow with any other part of his body."

"Gran!"

"He knew which side his bread was buttered, that's all I'm saying."

"I'm not sure I'm the marrying kind."

"Who said anything about marriage?"

Harry was confused. She was fairly certain that's exactly what Gran was talking about.

"I worry about you moving all the time," Gran said. "I'm not saying it's time to get tied down, but even a wanderer needs a home base."

"I have a home base. I just like to move it sometimes."

Gran gave her a gentle smile that made Harry want to wrap her in her arms. "It's hard to build a life when you don't put down roots, Harry."

"I have a life, Gran. I just like it unencumbered."

"As long as you're happy."

Harry spooned two scoops of tea into the pot and stared at the kettle, willing it to boil. She wanted to tell Gran everything about Tom's betrayal, about her unfair dismissal, about how lonely and desolate she'd felt before the call from Barbara had provided the chance to escape. But Harry was here to take care of Gran, not unload her troubles on her. If Harry told her everything, Gran would only worry.

"I am happy," she said. "Now, what do you fancy for breakfast?"

Harry opened the door of her grandmother's kitchen cupboard and stared in dismay at the jumbled contents. Faded spice jars, opened bags of flour, tins of fruit, beans, and fish stacked in teetering towers, and a plastic tub of something that might once have been glacé cherries. She glanced at her gran, suddenly understanding how much pain she must be in. Gran wasn't the type to let food go to waste, and disorganization was utterly unacceptable. If Gran had let her cupboards get this out of hand, she really must not be feeling herself.

"I really need to sort that out," Gran said, hobbling over and hanging her cane on the edge of the kitchen counter. "I just haven't been able to reach up there to straighten things up. I'll get the steps, shall I?"

"Why don't you just sit down, Gran?" Harry said, picturing her grandmother wobbling up her ancient step stool just as her hip gave out. "Drink your tea and you can catch me up on all the village gossip while I clean."

Harry hoped Gran's update would include Jamie Forrest. She wondered how long he'd been back in Hope, how he'd come to be dropping dinners in Gran's kitchen, and—if the topic came up—why there was no Mrs. Forrest or any mini Forrests. Now that she thought more about it, perhaps she wasn't the only one whose dreams had come off the rails. He was back here, too, after all.

Harry softened. She and Jamie had history. They were just kids back then—nothing serious—but she'd cared about him. Actually, he'd been her first real love, and she'd broken his heart. It was the right thing to do at the time, setting them both free to follow their dreams. But now that she'd experienced being dumped, she suffered a pang of guilt about Jamie.

"I can't sit idle while you do all the work," Gran said, plunking down with a poorly disguised groan onto a kitchen chair.

"You've got me all to yourself for three weeks, Gran, so you may as well take advantage of me. Once I go home, you can do it all yourself again. Meanwhile, you may as well make me a list of jobs, keep me out of trouble."

Truth was, it had shocked Harry to see how much her grandmother had aged. Gran had always been a force to be reckoned with, flitting through life like a woman twenty years younger. Under a bed sheet in the hallway was a purple titanium-framed road bike with components that even Harry could tell were high end. In the twenty-four hours since Harry had arrived, her grandmother had received visitors from the village ladies' group, the walking club, and the woman who taught belly dancing at the village hall where her grandmother had apparently been her star pupil. What Harry's mother, Barbara, had lacked in drive and determination, Gran had more than made up for.

When Harry had visited her grandmother as a child, she had always looked forward to cresting the hill above Hope and seeing the village for the first time. It had seemed to Harry like a fairytale place, the kind of place where adventures happened in books: Neverland, Narnia, Oz, Hope. She loved the way the little cottages clustered together around the village green, the narrow lanes like little tendrils reaching out into the countryside beyond. Here, everyone remembered her name, even though they saw her only once or twice a year. She had been safe here as a child.

But that had changed on the day she had *moved* to Hope. That day the village had seemed like the end of the line, the last-resort landing spot for two messed up lives. Harry's first stepfather, Tony, had left them. There'd been no yelling and accusations, no mounting tension in the house. Harry had come home from school one day to find her mother at the kitchen table, halfway through a bottle of expensive wine.

"Tony's left us," Barbara had said. "Found himself a new family. It's just us now."

And for six months, they had gone on without him. It was as if Harry's stepfather, the only father she'd ever known, had gone on a long business trip and not yet come back. Barbara seldom mentioned his name, certainly never talked about this new family. When Harry called her stepfather, he always answered his phone, talked to her as if nothing had changed, promised to explain everything to her when he saw her next. But he never made plans to come, and it didn't take long for Harry to understand that she was no longer part of his life.

Harry had just turned fifteen when she came home from school to find Barbara red-faced with rage. "Your stepfather has decided to starve us," she told Harry. "We can't possibly live on the money he's sending. We have no choice but to move in with my mother."

"That's okay," Harry had said, thinking of the little village and the chance for a fresh start. "It'll be an adventure."

"It will not be an adventure," Barbara said. "It will be the pinnacle of humiliation. You can't go home again, Harry. That's not how it works. You grow up, you move away, you make a life for yourself. You appreciate your parents for all they've done for you, but the goal of every parent is to prepare their child to fly the nest. When a child comes home, that means everyone has failed."

Harry had been stunned at the ferocity of Barbara's conviction. She didn't want her mother to be a failure in anyone's eyes. And Harry didn't want people to think of her that way either. "But it won't be forever," she said. "It's just temporary, isn't it? Just until…"

But she didn't know how to finish the sentence. Just until what? Tony wasn't coming back; her mother had never had to support herself, as far as Harry knew. And suddenly the village didn't feel like the place for a fresh start; it felt like the last resort.

But Harry had been wrong. And even though she had lived in her grandma's house for only a few years, it was the one place, of all the places she'd lived, that had ever truly felt like home. Barbara, who'd never been what you'd call a solid mother figure, had completely fallen apart when she found herself a single woman again. So, when she met Graham, a London financier, she'd hurried into another partnership.

"I'm not like you, Harry," Barbara had told her. "You're strong and independent. You have an amazing life ahead of you. I don't have the same opportunities."

Harry understood, or at least she'd said she did, but she'd refused to be shunted off again, arguing that it would harm her education to move schools now, and she'd be better off staying here with Gran.

With barely any hesitation, Barbara said, "Okay."

Something deep inside Harry had twanged, leaving her torn between feeling abandoned and relieved that Barbara wasn't forcing her to go. Harry would do better under Gran's gentle, loving care, anyway. She could finish school, be with Jamie, stay in this place where she'd been happy.

And she swore there and then she would never do what Barbara had done. If she ever had a daughter of her own, she vowed never to abandon her. And she promised she would never drop everything, never tip her life on its head, never compromise her own future for a man.

It was afternoon by the time Harry finished the cupboard and stepped back to admire her handiwork. With all the out-of-date spices and half-used baking ingredients gone, the cupboard was now less than a quarter full. Harry noted that it still contained more than her own kitchen cabinets.

"I don't need it anyway," Gran said. "I've got Jamie's meals now."

Harry's ears perked up. "What about them?"

Gran gushed on about how she'd long ago given up cooking and was practically living on sandwiches before she heard about Jamie's service. "I make them two at a time so I don't have to cook every day."

"I was surprised to see Jamie here," Harry ventured, trying to sound casual. "I thought he had a big, fancy restaurant in London."

"He did for a while, and then he came back. Lucky for us."

"But he had so much potential," Harry said.

"And he's using it. His kits are a hit. Everyone loves him."

"But...," Harry began, then closed her mouth. Who was she to give a lecture on success, especially given her recent career "triumph"? The difference was, he had returned home and stayed; she would keep moving forward. "Good for him," is all she said.

Gran looked tired. She didn't have to tell Harry that it was hard on her hip to stand for long periods. She didn't put up much of a fight when Harry suggested she put up her feet for an hour before dinner.

"I'll see to these," Harry said, pulling the boxed meals from the fridge and reading "salmon *en croute*" from the label.

"I didn't think you liked to cook."

It was true. Harry had never had any interest in learning to cook. Gran had insisted she teach Harry enough basics so she could make eggs or boil pasta, but beyond that, Harry didn't care.

"Come on," Harry said. "Even I can follow instructions."

"If you're sure it's no trouble," Gran said, and hobbled into the living room. Harry helped her down on to the narrow gray couch and draped a cashmere pashmina over her for warmth—no crocheted throws for Gran, thought Harry. She went back to the kitchen and poured herself a glass of wine, put on Gran's apron—one of those plastic-coated gag aprons with a woman's body clad in lingerie, with two tasseled pasties dangling from the breasts—and set about warming up the salmon *en croute* that Jamie had brought.

But when Harry opened the box, expecting to find two trays of salmon *en croute* and directions on how to re-heat them in the microwave, she found two pieces of raw salmon, a packet of some green fronded herb, raw potatoes, a roll of pastry, a plastic tub of butter, and three sachets of spices. She pulled out the recipe card. Along with a photo of a fillet of salmon, washed in a creamy dill sauce and topped with a golden crust of pastry, were step-by-step instructions. Harry realized, with growing dread, that she would have to build this culinary wonder herself. Under her breath, she cursed Jamie Forrest. Why could he not have gone the extra step and prepared the meals himself? He was a chef, wasn't he? What kind of chef prepped all the food and then didn't bother to cook it? Harry sighed, lifted the ingredients from the box, and pre-heated the oven, per the first step in the instructions.

Harry expected to see some familiar faces in Hope. The village was like that, full of people whose families had lived there for generations. In the past few years, according to Gran, an influx of new people moving out from the cities had driven up the prices in appealing villages like Hope. But Harry also knew that many of the young people she'd known as a teenager had left and moved to places with jobs. That Jamie, with his big aspirations, came back to Hope surprised her.

She laughed to herself now about seeing Jamie on Gran's doorstep. How many times had she opened the door to him like that? How many times had Gran called up the stairs to say he was here, and Harry had come down to find him cooking at Gran's stove? They were so young and full of big dreams then. Harry saw hers through, though. She'd gone to university, got her degree, found her dream job, moved far away from Hope, built a life for herself. She assumed Jamie had done the same, built his life far away, gained the success she always believed he'd achieve. But somehow they'd both ended up back here. Had she turned into her mother, after all? God, she hoped not. No, definitely not. Harry was not Barbara. Harry did not come back to Hope because her life was falling apart. She came to help her Gran. That was all.

But as Harry opened the ingredients and laid them out on the counter, she was forced to admit that there were some similarities in her and her mother's returns to Hope. Both discovered cheating men, both had been jobless, and both returned to Hope to lick their wounds. The big difference, Harry told herself, was that unlike Barbara she would stay only a few short weeks, long enough to help Gran. And unlike Barbara, she would pick up the pieces of her life and put them solidly back together again. Unlike Barbara, she would not fall apart.

CHAPTER FOUR

JAMIE SLUMPED at Michael's kitchen table, trying to keep his mind on the details of his friend's upcoming wedding. Jamie was catering the reception and he was looking forward to the challenge, not to mention the opportunity to cook. But now his mind was everywhere except on smoked salmon blinis and goat cheese puffs.

"Sarah's getting the final numbers," Michael said. "Just waiting for her friend to confirm. She's single, by the way."

"Sarah?" Jamie asked, rejoining the conversation from his thoughts about Harry Belmont.

"Carmen. Sarah's friend?"

"Right. Sorry," said Jamie, picking at a knot in the rough oak surface of the table.

"You all right?" Michael asked.

Jamie waved him off. He was here to talk about the wedding plans, not his issues of the heart, but running into Harry had knocked him off kilter. They were old news, and he had no interest in changing that. But then he'd given her his card, like some kind of invitation. "In case you need anything." Why did he always try to be helpful? And seeing her at her grandmother's—the place he'd first laid eyes on her—took him right back to those hazy summer days.

For Jamie, if not for Harry, it had been love at first sight. He'd been helping his dad prepare for the annual Midsummer Fair when a small moving van had pulled up outside Old Mrs. Belmont's cottage. A tall woman had climbed down from the driver's side, causing his dad to make a strange, strangled noise that sounded like "Barbara Belmont." Jamie was fifteen and fully aware of the allure of women of all ages, but it had been the first time he'd under-stood that his father had similar urges.

"Dad," he'd chided, elbowing his father in the ribs.

"Just looking," his dad said. "I wouldn't dream of touch-ing, not anymore. But once upon a time, Barbara Belmont was the prettiest girl in Hope. Broke every heart this side of the Pennines, and a few on the other side, I'd be willing to bet. I would have risked my heart for even a glance from that girl, but she never gave me the time of day. Then I met your mother and learned the difference between love and lust."

Jamie wasn't sure he wanted to hear any more about his parents' romance, and he elbowed his dad again. Ever since his dad had turned forty, he'd become soppy, wearing his heart on his sleeve and talking about things that made Jamie squirm. There were certain things you never wanted to know about your parents, and the trials of their early love lives was one of them. Still, he couldn't deny that Barbara Belmont was an attractive woman and he could see that she must have been a stunner in his dad's heyday.

He was just thinking about how he might never have been born if Barbara had given his dad a second look—or even a first look—when the van's passenger door swung open. A girl climbed down and stretched her arms above her head, revealing a tantalizing flash of skin above low-slung jeans that looked actually distressed, rather than bought for a mint that way. Jamie took in her lean body tanned to a copper brown, the glossy dark hair pulled into a ponytail, and the Game Boy stuffed into her back pocket, as if the world might get too boring for her at any moment. And then this vision of cool turned and saw him staring, and before he could collect himself and look away, she flashed him a smile that took his breath away. Her full lips parted to reveal straight healthy teeth, a smile so wide it forced dimples into the peachy soft skin of her cheeks. Jamie's dad might barely have registered as a blip on Barbara's radar, but Jamie was determined he would kiss that beautiful mouth of her daughter's.

And kiss it, he did. Eventually. After months of lingering in front of her grandmother's cottage like a hungry stray cat, Jamie finally got to kiss Harry. And, oh, did he ever? On her mouth, on her neck, on the tips of her fingers, on parts of her body that he'd never even imagined were accessible to kisses. Jamie could not believe his luck that Harry Belmont had chosen him. And for eighteen months, he was in love. *They* were in love. He knew because Harry told him so.

Then, as quickly as she had appeared in his life, she went away. A place at a university in Scotland for her, culinary school for him, their paths forking, and Harry deciding they should follow their dreams unencumbered. That's the word she'd used, as if Jamie was some heavy bundle she'd be forced to haul around. And Jamie, foolish Jamie, had kept the candle burning, sure she'd come back for him eventually. Instead, she moved further away. America, he heard through the village grapevine. Harry hadn't just broken Jamie's heart; she had first constructed it to a design that fit only her, and then she had gone and left his Harry-shaped heart behind. Try as he might—and he had tried—Jamie had never found anyone else to fill the hole that Harry had built. Not even Alexis.

And now she was back. For a month. A little door in Jamie's Harry-shaped heart creaked open. He peered inside, remembered the feel of her skin, the sound of her laughter, the warmth of her love. He sank into it for a brief moment, then slammed the door shut.

"Jamie?" Michael's voice broke into his memory. "Where've you been, mate?"

Jamie looked at the friend he'd known since they were scruffy little boys. Both had grown up, moved away, and returned to Hope. Michael had come back for a simple life, a life that he was now planning to share with Sarah. Jamie had come back because he'd trusted the wrong person in business. Just like he'd trusted the wrong person with his heart all those years ago.

"Lot on my mind," Jamie said. "One of those weeks."

"Did you set up those interviews yet?"

"Next thing on my list."

"If I didn't know you better, I'd think you were procrastinating."

Jamie shook his head. "Just busy."

"Which is why you need to hire."

"No one is going to do the job better than me, though," Jamie said.

Michael laughed. "Of course they won't. But honestly, mate, how good a job are you doing by trying to do it alone?"

"You're lucky," Jamie said. "You have Sarah."

"Luckiest man alive," Michael said. "But sooner or later, you're going to have to trust someone again."

"Yeah," said Jamie. "I will." He pushed up from the table. "Tell Sarah not to worry. I'll make sure everything about the wedding is perfect."

Michael clapped him on the back. "You're a good friend."

"Yeah," Jamie said, and hurried out to his van before his friend could peer further into his soul and tell him truths about himself.

He checked the route map Ollie had sent and put the van into gear, focusing his mind on his last customer. He had to admit that Ollie's route mapping program had sped up his deliveries that day. But the new route took him right past Mrs. Belmont's cottage and increased his chances of running into Harry again. And that was something he didn't want to do.

Ignoring the map, he flicked on the van's left turn signal and headed to the junction of a small, winding lane. It would take him along the hillside above Hope, past the old stone circle, and down behind the church, entering the village from the opposite end and thus avoiding Harry. It was a ridiculous route, but well worth it, as far as Jamie was concerned. He didn't need Harry Belmont reminding him of all his life's mistakes and all her great successes.

He had barely made the turn when his phone rang. He clicked the hands-free button on the dash and answered.

"You've gone off-piste, Bossman," Ollie said, sounding like a stern teacher.

"I'm running a personal errand," Jamie lied.

"Right. But you have a route mapped back to base camp and you've gone off track."

"It's only a detour."

"If we're going to test this, Bossman, you have to trust the directions."

"Yeah, but..."

"You promised you'd test it."

Jamie sighed. "I did."

"So...?"

"I'll turn around, Ollie, Okay? I'll follow the route."

"Nice work, Bossman. I'll adjust your minor detour when you get back."

Jamie slowed the van and pulled across to a wide gate leading into a field. He did a quick three-point turn in the lane and headed back the way he'd come. He was beginning to wonder who was in charge of this operation. And if he hired more staff, that would just be more people to manage, more people he'd need to trust.

Jamie saw the smoke the second he turned into the village. Try as he might, he could not look away from Mrs. Belmont's cottage, so he spotted the plume of black smoke curling from the back of the house right away. He gunned the van to the opposite side of the street, earning himself a honk from a passing car. He screeched to a haphazard halt and abandoned the van at the curb.

"Oy, you can't park like that, mate," someone yelled, but Jamie didn't stop to argue. He sprinted up the path of Mrs. Belmont's cottage and yanked open the kitchen door. Smoke billowed out, losing him for a moment in its foggy grip. Why were there no smoke alarms sounding? Why were there no sirens racing to the emergency? He pictured Mrs. Belmont unconscious on the floor of her smoke-filled living room. And then he pictured Harry beside her. His heart skipped a beat. He had to save them. He couldn't let Harry die.

But as the smoke escaped through the open back door, a

silhouette emerged from the gloom. Something flicked in front of his face and, as the smoke cleared, he saw Harry wafting a dish towel. And then the unmistakable smell of burnt pastry reached his nose.

"Please tell me that isn't your cooking," he said, his nose twitching from the pungent air.

"It *is* my cooking, but it's *your* recipe," Harry said, thrusting her hands to her hips.

With the air in the kitchen now cleared, he could see a baking tray on the stove. On it were what appeared to be two lumps of coal. Underneath the charcoal smell was a vague aroma of fish. "Is that my salmon *en croute?*"

"No," said Harry. "It's my salmon en funeral pyre."

Jamie stared at the incinerated bricks. "What happened?"

"I followed the directions."

Jamie grabbed the recipe card. His salmon *en croute* was a firm favorite with his customers, and no one had ever complained that the directions were wrong. "You baked it for twenty minutes at Gas Mark 7, then twenty at Gas Mark 4."

"No," Harry said. "I did it for forty minutes at 7, like it says."

Jamie blinked at the recipe card, trying to understand where Harry had seen this instruction. "It says right here in step four: Bake for twenty minutes at Gas Mark 7; lower heat to Gas Mark 4, and bake another twenty minutes."

Harry grabbed the card and peered at it. "Yes, but here at the top it says: 'Cooking time: 40 minutes.' And here in step 2 it says: 'Pre-heat oven to Gas Mark 7.'"

Jamie grabbed it back. "But here in step four it says to turn the oven *down.*"

Harry rolled her eyes. "Well, who has time to read all

those piddly little details? I'm busy. When I come home from work, I need to get food on the table. I can't be messing around reading twenty-nine steps of instructions."

"There are six steps."

"Whatever. I don't have time for cooking."

"So, what do you eat? I thought you said you ordered meal kits."

"I do," Harry said. "But my meal kits come with two steps. One: remove meal from packaging. Two: Heat for however many minutes. I stick it in the microwave, set the timer, go for a shower, and by the time I come out, *voilà*, my dinner is cooked to perfection."

Jamie felt his lip curl at the idea of a microwaved dinner, but he pulled it back in line. "When was the last time you had a home-cooked meal, Harry?"

Harry screwed up her face as if she was looking way, way back into the dim and distant past for a long-forgotten memory.

"That long, eh?" Jamie asked.

"I eat out a lot."

"Well, why don't you have a seat and let me treat you and your gran to one now?"

Harry glanced at the ruined dinner. "I don't think even you could rescue that."

"I've got extra kits in the van. I can even make you enough to have cold leftovers for lunch. My treat. You won't regret it, I promise." And before Harry could object, Jamie slipped out of the kitchen and back down the path. He grabbed his last delivery from the van and ran three doors down to drop it off. Only when he'd straightened out the van and pulled out two chilled salmon *en croute* kits did he think that cooking dinner for Harry Belmont felt an awful lot like dropping his heart into a meat grinder. Too late now, though. Because Jamie had promised, and he always kept his promises.

Jamie moved around Mrs. Belmont's kitchen feeling completely at home. It had been more than ten years since he'd cooked here, but his hands seemed to remember where everything was. He reached for the knife block with one hand, found scissors in a drawer with the other, and reached for a wooden spatula held in a terra-cotta jar on the counter, without even looking. And all the while he kept his eyes firmly *off* Harry.

"Watching you cook is like watching a ballet," Harry said.

"You go to the ballet a lot?" Jamie thought that didn't sound like Harry's thing, at least not the Harry he remembered. But people changed. Didn't they?

"Just once. In San Francisco."

She went quiet then, her eyes drifting up to the corner of the kitchen. Jamie glanced at her, wondering who she'd been with. Someone special? Someone still special? It must have been an excellent memory, because she disappeared into her thoughts. He turned his attention back to the salmon, laying it on the pastry in front of him, sure now that Harry had left behind someone else.

"It's just a matter of paying attention to what's going on around you," Jamie said.

Harry's head snapped up. "What?"

"Cooking. Once you start, it's a matter of focus. You sort of get in the zone. The prep's the worst bit. It's time-consuming; that's why people love the kits."

"But your business is just the prep part, and it's clear you still love the cooking part, too," Harry said.

Jamie shrugged. "I had my fun creating the recipes. And I like doing the deliveries; I like talking to people."

"You always did. I think you were in every club in school."

Jamie laughed. "Even the Computer Club, although I only joined that because of you."

"Me?"

"Yeah. I loved watching you find solutions. You had a way of looking at things beyond what was in front of you."

He turned away then and moved around the stove, stirring and tasting. He wished he hadn't said that. Because Harry had looked ahead to a future without him, and he'd enjoyed nothing about watching that.

"You were going to open a restaurant," Harry said. "And you did, didn't you? In London?"

"Yeah, well, I never did have your head for business."

"It didn't work out?"

"Let's just say I don't have a talent for picking partners."

"At least not business partners."

Jamie didn't answer. He didn't have a knack for picking any kind of partner other than the perfect sides to go with his main dishes, but he would not admit that to Harry. Jamie plated the perfect golden-brown salmon *en croute*, placed a fan of tender asparagus beside each, and drizzled it with a light, creamy sauce, all the while aware of Harry's eyes on him. He wiped the rim of the plates like a pro and set one plate in front of Harry and the other for her grandmother. "I should go," he said.

"Why don't you stay? Gran eats like a bird, so we can share a plate. She'd love to have you eat with us." When he hesitated, she added. "So would I."

Jamie blinked, unsure how to answer. Was Harry Belmont flirting with him? If so, his instincts urged him to run. "That would be nice," he said, kicking himself even as the words came out.

"Perfect. I'll get Gran."

The nap must have done Harry's gran a world of good, because she never stopped talking throughout the entire meal. Jamie answered her questions between bites of his salmon *en croute*. He seldom ate his own meal kits, and he hadn't tasted this dish since he'd first created it. A layer of spinach and watercress mix split the pink fish, all of it wrapped in a thin crust of pastry that flaked just so. He smeared a bit of the dill sauce over it and popped it into his mouth. The sharp horseradish in the sauce cut the oiliness of the salmon, and the watercress added a nice pepperiness to the spinach. But the sauce needed something more. He rolled the flavors slowly over his tastebuds, trying to feel the missing flavor.

"You should think about opening a restaurant here," Harry said, interrupting his thoughts. "It's the perfect spot for a cozy bistro and you would probably get enough tourists passing through to keep up a steady business."

"Dill," Jamie said.

"Dill?"

"The sauce needs more dill. I should update the recipe."

"Well, update the instructions while you're at it, so a non-cook like me can follow along."

Jamie wrinkled his nose. How could someone as brilliant as Harry, someone who worked with code and data and logic, for goodness' sake, be unable to follow a simple recipe?

"You can't open a restaurant," Mrs. Belmont said. "What am I going to do without my Local Goodness kits?"

"Once you get your new hip, you'll be able to walk to

Jamie's restaurant," Harry said. "And you'll be able to get all your favorite meals cooked for you."

Jamie's head was spinning. More dill, retest all the recipes, update the instructions so that even Harry could follow them. Open a restaurant. Get back in the kitchen and create again. Share his passion for food with others. A restaurant. It had always been his dream. Why not open a place right here in Hope?

He shook his head. There went Harry and her big ideas again, getting into his brain and complicating everything. "Your gran's right. I have enough on my plate with Local Goodness. People depend on me now. I have an employee, too. For my sins."

"That boy Ollie," Gran said. "He's a clever lad, that one."

"Too clever sometimes. He's determined to run my business for me."

"Maybe you should let him," said Harry. "Go back to what you really love."

"He's not ready for that."

"You can teach people skills, Jamie, but you can't teach passion. And you always had that. If he's not the right person for the job, let him go and find someone who is."

Jamie stared at Harry. "I can't just 'let him go;' he depends on me. Maybe in California you can come and go from jobs as you please, but it's not so easy here. There aren't too many opportunities here in Hope."

"But Ollie's young. He could move to the city, find more opportunities."

Jamie's jaw clenched. It was so easy for Harry. She was like the beech trees that grew in the nearby woods—solid and strong (and yes, lovely to look at), but with roots that were shallow. If she chose, she could uproot and move on a whim, settle her roots again and bloom where she was planted. She could make new friends, build a sort of family, make a home wherever she was. But people like him and Ollie weren't like that. They were more like oaks that could withstand all kinds of weather, but were happiest in one place. Jamie loved the familiarity of the village, the faces he'd known for years, the friends like Michael who could finish his sentences. Not that Harry was cold or didn't get attached to people, not at all. But she could leave her past behind. She'd certainly had no trouble leaving him.

"I should go soon," Jamie said, taking his plate to the sink. "Let me do these dishes and I'll leave you ladies to get your beauty sleep."

"You cooked. I'll wash," Harry said.

She slid in beside him at the sink, rolling up her sleeves. Jamie felt the warmth of her body next to his, the scent of her in his nose. The little crack in Jamie's heart, the one he was so sure had healed, suddenly ached, and he feared it might open again.

He grabbed his jacket and hurried for the door.

"Thanks for dinner, Mrs. B. Hope your op goes well. Let me know if you need anything."

And with that, he slipped out the door.

Once outside, the cool evening air felt like a bucket of ice water tipped over his head. He blinked and shook away the soft warmth of Harry's voice, the sensation of her standing next to him at the sink. The reality check was just what he needed. It was so typical of Harry to put career before people, just like she'd done with him. But Jamie wasn't like that.

He stuck his hands in his jacket pockets and stalked out to his van. Open a restaurant? He couldn't even open a folder to look at job applications. And now he'd wasted a whole evening and was still no closer to hiring help. She was right about one thing, though. Maybe he should train Ollie. He could use the app to do the deliveries his way, and Jamie would never have to see Harry Belmont and her crazy ideas again.

CHAPTER FIVE

TWO DAYS LATER, Harry kissed Gran on her soft cheek and handed her over to a waiting nurse.

"Don't get into any trouble while I'm away," Gran said.

"Don't you either," Harry said.

Gran laughed, then flinched with pain. As the nurse wheeled Gran off to pre-op, a sense of the ground teetering beneath her overcame Harry. She didn't want to see Gran go, but couldn't bear to see her in pain. She was glad to have some time to herself, but terrified in case she never saw her Gran again. Her heart pulled this way and that, and Harry had to fight to keep unexpected tears at bay. She had the sense of grieving the loss of her gran before she was even gone.

Outside the hospital, she pulled out her phone, desperate for an understanding ear. But who could she call? She'd told her mother she'd call once Gran was out of surgery. But, even if she wasn't floating around the Med on a luxury yacht, Barbara was the last person Harry would call for comfort.

It was one o'clock in the morning in San Francisco. It

was possible her friend Soraya would still be up, but unlikely on a Tuesday. Her friend Kate had transferred to New York City a couple of months earlier, and four a.m. was definitely too early to call her. She looked at her phone and scrolled through her recent calls—Judith, the taxi, the hospital. She didn't need a service, though. She needed a friend.

Harry's thoughts flitted to Jamie. He would understand how worried she was about Gran. She kicked herself for leaving his card on Gran's table, determined to avoid him, but a quick search turned up the Local Goodness website and phone number. Her finger hovered for a moment. She couldn't call Jamie. She couldn't fall back on his kindness every time she wanted someone to care. Not when she'd hurt him. Not when she'd barely given him a thought in all the years since she'd left.

She'd thought about him all the time when she first moved away from Hope at eighteen, leaving him behind to study business and computer science at Heriot-Watt University in Edinburgh. She'd been young and headstrong, so determined to move forward and never look back, to do whatever it took to make sure she didn't become her mother.

She'd vowed not to call Jamie, but one day, a couple of months after she'd left Hope, she'd broken down. When he'd offered to make the trip from London, where he was enrolled in culinary school, to visit her for the weekend, she'd agreed. "Just as friends," she'd said.

She'd met him at the station and they spent the day wandering the streets of Edinburgh, visiting the castle, and hiking up to Arthur's seat. They headed back to campus in the evening and went down to the Student Union Bar. There they'd danced. God, how they'd danced. Every time Harry thought she was ready to sit the next song out, the DJ played an old favorite and Harry and Jamie had stayed on the dance floor until their clothes were damp with sweat and their hair clung to their clammy faces.

They'd staggered back to the dorms and collapsed into Harry's narrow bed, exhausted, but still laughing and talking about the night.

"It's been boring as anything without you," Jamie said.

"You live in one of the most exciting cities on Earth," Harry said. "How can you be bored?"

"I miss you," Jamie said.

In a small corner of her brain, a little voice of reason reminded Harry that she and Jamie had broken up. It explained that kissing him now would be a terrible idea. But she did it anyway. "I've missed you, too," she said. And that had been true.

Kissing Jamie again had felt like being home, and Harry had been homesick. Jamie's kisses warmed her, sent little fingers all down her body, making her stomach tighten, making her thighs clench. She'd found a gap beneath his shirt and run her hands over his damp skin, feeling his body tighten at her touch. Her limbs went loose and her jaw, tense from the stress of finding her way in the strange new world of student life, relaxed. When Jamie kissed her that night, she had melted into the bed, softened to fit him, molded as she'd pressed his familiar body against hers.

She helped him take off her shirt, planted lines of tiny kisses on his neck as he unsnapped her bra, her breasts responding to the sudden chill of the air and the tender touch of his mouth. When they made love that night, there was no awkwardness. They knew one another's bodies, what each of them liked best. Harry arched to move closer to him, felt the tautness of his legs, the rough feel of the hairs against her smooth skin contrasting with the smoothness of his fingertips as they ran down her side.

She had cried as they fell together, partly in ecstasy but mostly from realizing that she had let Jamie go. In that moment, Harry had felt whole again in a way she hadn't since she'd left Hope. And Jamie had lain beside her, their feet touching. Sweet, gentle Jamie. Everything so right.

But by morning, everything was wrong. Harry had woken feeling like a double-decker bus had run her over. Her head throbbed and her body ached. And there was Jamie, his hair looking like a squirrel's nest, his breath hot and stale, his body flung across hers, pinning her to the bed. Everything comfortable, everything wrong. She allowed one last wave of contentment to wash over her, then slid out of the bed.

In the shower, she'd scrubbed away the emotional mess and let the logic shine through. Jamie wasn't her future. They were eighteen, had their whole lives ahead of them. Hadn't they talked this through already? They weren't ready to settle down, to compromise for one another. There'd be plenty of time ahead for that. Yes, she loved Jamie. Yes, he was wonderful in every way. If it was meant to be, they'd find their way back to one another, but they both had futures to build first. If Harry let herself fall back in love with Jamie then, she knew she'd be making compromises in her life forever. And so would he.

In the shower that morning, she had scrubbed clean all the places Jamie had touched just a few hours before. She'd rinsed the suds away and turned the water cold, giving herself one last blast of pragmatism. And then she'd told Jamie it was time to go.

Now, outside the hospital, she regretted not treating Jamie's heart more gently, the way he had always treated hers. Calling him now would feel like using him, and she never wanted to do that again.

Instead, she rang for a taxi and went home to Gran's empty cottage. She busied herself, hoping to take her mind off Gran and focusing instead on rebuilding her life. She sent her updated resume to the agency, mentioning that she was open to relocating for the right opportunity. She emailed half a dozen contacts in her network, letting them know she was in the market for a new opportunity, wording her emails carefully so as not to imply she was desperate. It was too soon to worry—she had sought-after skills and a solid track record—but the time with Gran would go quickly and although her savings would carry her for a good six months, she needed to get back to work soon. More than that, she needed to reboot her life.

Still, she couldn't concentrate on the task at hand. Every few minutes she checked her phone again, waiting for an update on her gran. She knew Gran was strong and way too feisty to let something like a hip operation derail her, but things happened and Harry couldn't bear the thought of losing her.

Desperate to talk to someone, Harry called her mother. The call went to voicemail. No longer able to focus on her job search, Harry found a feather duster under Gran's sink and set about dusting the house. Anything to take her mind off worrying.

Gran's house was surprisingly modern. She had a cozy gray settee and two mismatched chairs arranged around a simple white fireplace. The mantlepiece displayed a tasteful collection of green glass vases, the tallest of which held a sprig of bright ceramic poppies. On one of the pale sage walls, a giant pocket watch ticked loudly in the silence. Gran had arranged a cashmere blanket and a collection of bright pillows on the couch to give the whole place a cozy feel.

But in between the carefully chosen design elements, Harry's duster discovered some ancient treasures she'd all but forgotten. In one corner was an ancient metal waste bin. It had been red once, with pictures of kittens around the outside. It had faded so much that it blended in with the muted colors of the room. Harry had loved those kittens, with their marmalade fur and bright blue eyes. In the top of a kitchen cabinet, Harry found an old tea service that had belonged to her great-grandmother, and possibly her mother before her. Harry recalled the china roses and silver rim of the saucers. As she moved upstairs to dust the shelves and dresser, she knew instinctively which stairs would creak. As a teenager, she'd used this knowledge to sneak in late, hoping, but usually failing, that she wouldn't wake her gran. In a cabinet underneath the bathroom sink, Harry found a familiar plastic jug. It had the logo for a powdered milk brand on the side, but was now relegated to some unpleasant bathroom task. But Harry had a sudden recollection of long walks in the countryside with Gran, of stopping at a pretty spot to eat the sandwiches and crisps they'd packed. She remembered Gran pulling out a thermos of scalding water and making two cups of tea, stirring in the granules of powdered milk that always seemed to float on the top. Gran insisting that tea tasted better out in the fresh air, floating milk granules notwithstanding. So many fond memories.

Jamie had implied that it had been easy for Harry to uproot her life and move away, but he was wrong. Yes, as a fresh graduate with a career ahead, moving to another country had been a big adventure, an opportunity too good to pass up. She hadn't planned to stay and build a life there.

At twenty-two, everything had been about the now; she hadn't thought about "forever."

The cost of moving so far from her family had seemed small at first. She'd learned to navigate a new culture and the small, but potentially embarrassing, differences in language. Sometimes she felt left out when people talked about childhood memories that she didn't share. She hadn't grown up with the same TV shows, or music, or snacks, so when people said, "Remember when...," Harry didn't remember at all.

But as Gran aged, the price became higher. How many times had Harry wished she could pop over to take Gran to a doctor's appointment, help her in her garden, or wake up on Christmas morning in the familiar house? But she'd always been too busy, her work creeping in to fill every spare corner of her life.

She recalled her co-worker, Jasmine, who'd grown up in the Philippines, being so astounded to learn that Harry's grandmother lived alone, that her mother had a life far away, that Harry had stayed away for so long and not moved back to care for her family.

"My gran's fine on her own," Harry had said, but the conversation had left her wondering who had it right, the Western culture that encouraged children to fly the nest, only to find themselves alone, or the cultures that valued elders and whose younger generations adjusted their own lives to make sure their parents and grandparents had care.

Jamie had made her sound so cold, like moving away had never even fazed her. And he'd acted so strangely the other night. Harry ran the conversation over and over in her head, trying to pinpoint exactly what she'd said that had upset him. She wondered if perhaps his business was struggling, that letting Ollie go had been on his mind. Or maybe the restaurant was a sore point for him. Clearly his former partner had burned him. Harry wondered what had happened.

Jamie was so talented. Even when they were young and believed anything was possible, even when they'd talked about their big dreams, he had never truly understood the depths of his creative talents. She could see why he resisted starting a restaurant in Hope. It was a small village with a light tourist trade and already had a pub that served decent food. He needed to think bigger, spread his wings, but he was stuck here, and it was too late. His roots were down way too deep, and there was no way he'd move now.

Despite not being close to Gran, Harry knew she had been right to leave all those years ago. Hadn't she? Without the complications of love, she'd launched her life, firing into the professional stratosphere and landing on the other side of the globe in a world she had only imagined. And Jamie had been free to follow his dreams. So the restaurant hadn't worked out. But if she'd been part of his life, would he even have tried? Their lives would have been smaller if they'd embarked on them together. Letting Jamie go had been the right thing to do for both of them. She was convinced of it.

She checked her phone. Still no word about Gran. She clicked on her contacts and tried her friends. The call to Kate went to voicemail; Soraya answered, but said she couldn't talk now. It did not surprise Harry that Taz didn't answer. The fourth call got her mother's voicemail again.

On the kitchen table sat Jamie's business card. "In case you need anything," he'd said. Her finger hovered over Jamie's name. She did need something. She took a breath and called.

CHAPTER SIX

JAMIE WAS NERVOUS. Maybe he shouldn't have sent Ollie out on the deliveries. Ollie wasn't stupid—far from it—in fact Jamie wondered if he might be verging on genius. Ollie didn't think like other people. His mind seemed to go off on tangents, even though it somehow came back to the key problem and always with a solution. But Jamie worried his deliveries might go on similar tangents, and he couldn't afford any more mistakes. He hoped Ollie would stay focused on testing his own routing program and follow the instructions to the letter. If so, it would give Jamie a few free hours to work on his recipes.

Ever since his dinner with Harry and her grandmother, Jamie had been thinking about cooking. Obviously, he couldn't open a restaurant. He'd thought about it, though. He'd walked slowly past the former village shop that had once sold every household item a person could imagine. It had stood empty for several months now, which caused Jamie to think that Hope wasn't the place to launch a business venture, no matter what Harry Belmont thought. Harry had always had big, wild dreams, but she wasn't great when it came to practicality. You couldn't just "open a restaurant" on a whim. It took analysis and planning, investment, a solid plan—all the stuff guaranteed to kill any creative spark. But she'd been right about his need to cook again. It was time he tried some new creations, time to update his menu options.

He turned on some music, shook out his shoulders and moved around a kitchen.

"Like watching a ballet," Harry had said when he'd cooked at her grandmother's.

He laughed. Now that he was back in the kitchen, the ideas flowed again. A mushroom grower he bought from had recently introduced some new varieties to her list, and Jamie had ideas on how to use them. A long-time customer had reduced her order after the family had decided to eat vegan twice a week. This could be an opportunity to offer vegan and vegetarian selections, maybe even other dietary options, like gluten-free or Paleo. He'd done some research on the vegan diet and was looking forward to the challenge of creating new recipes, starting with a vegan mushroom stroganoff.

He was just stirring in some sherry and adjusting the recipe when his phone rang. Normally, he would turn off his phone while creating, so he could focus on his work, but with Ollie out on deliveries, he needed to be available. He glanced at the screen, hoping it wasn't Ollie. It wasn't; it was a funny number with too many digits. Someone calling from overseas.

Jamie wiped his hands on his kitchen towel and let the phone ring again. What if it was Harry? After she'd been so pushy with her business ideas, she was about the last person he wanted interrupting his work. But the truth was, Harry had lit a fire in him again—not that kind of fire, of course, but a fire for cooking—and he wanted to tell her. What he didn't want was another lecture on how to live his life. He let the phone ring again.

But Mrs. Belmont's operation was today. What if something had gone wrong? Jamie grabbed the phone and stabbed at the Answer icon.

"Harry?" he said. "Is everything okay?"

There was silence at the end of the phone. Jamie's stomach dropped. He'd known Mrs. Belmont since he was a boy. In some ways she had replaced his own grandmother, who had died when he was young, and even after Harry was no longer in his life, Mrs. Belmont had remained. If anything happened to her...

"Harry," he said again.

Finally, Harry spoke. Her voice was timid and uncertain, a world away from the confident woman he'd encountered in her gran's kitchen. "Are you busy?"

Jamie glanced at his butcher block prep table. Dishes of ingredients sat ready to be cooked, sprigs of rosemary needed chopping. On the stove, the mushrooms simmered in their sauce and a pot of salted water bubbled away, waiting for the pasta to be added. Beside the stove, his notebook lay open to a page covered in scrawled notes and crossed out quantities. "Not busy," he said. "What's wrong?"

"Nothing." Harry didn't sound convincing. "Nothing's wrong. Gran's in surgery and I... It's silly. I just needed to hear a reassuring voice, and I thought of you."

"Come over here," Jamie said, before he could stop himself.

"You're busy."

"I could use some help," Jamie said, an idea popping into his head. "You can't sit home alone worrying."

"If you're sure you don't mind."

"As long as you're hungry."

He hung up the phone, tasted the mushrooms, added a quarter teaspoon of salt and an extra dash of sherry, and adjusted the recipe in his notebook. By the time Harry arrived, the stroganoff was ready. He served up a bowl for her and, even though it was barely noon, offered her a glass of burgundy to go with it.

"Your gran's going to be fine, you know," Jamie said, as Harry blew on the rich gravy in her spoon.

"I know. I just feel so helpless."

"You're used to things being in your control, and this isn't."

Harry tried to smile, but it faltered halfway and faded. "I'm not sure anything is in my control anymore."

Jamie served himself a bowl and slid in beside her. "You'll forgive me if I'm prying, but I was surprised to see you here. So was your gran. If you want to talk, I'm still a good listener, you know."

Harry closed her eyes, and he wondered what she was thinking about, if she was lining up the right words to say what was on her mind. "This is really good, you know," she said.

Jamie waited. He had so many questions about how Harry had spent the last decade, but he sensed if he gave her space, she'd open up sooner or later.

HARRY FELT BETTER ALREADY. The mushroom stroganoff was savory and comforting, melting away some of the anxiety she'd felt about her gran. But a fresh worry wormed its way in. Jamie was being kind, offering to listen while she talked, but she needed to keep her guard up. No way was she about to spill her life story and all its recent catastrophes.

She smiled, careful not to meet his gaze. "Everything's fine with me, but tell me about you. When did move back here?"

Now it was Jamie's turn to look away. "Five years ago, thereabouts."

"Didn't care for London?"

"I loved London, the city at least."

"But?"

"The restaurant business was pretty cutthroat. It wasn't for me and I knew almost right away."

"But your place was doing really well, wasn't it? Gran sent me a clipping from the paper."

"Slate." Jamie wrinkled his nose. "It was doing great. But my partner and I had different visions. She had big dreams."

Harry tried to hide her surprise. *She*. Now she thought about it, the clipping Gran had sent had included a picture of Jamie and a woman with a dazzling smile and a mass of shiny black curls. Harry wondered—not exactly idly—if they'd ever been more than just business partners, but she chided herself. Not everyone was foolish enough to mix business and pleasure. Not everyone was like her. "But you had big dreams, too."

"I did, but we had different versions of the same dream. She wanted to be a famous chef, and I just wanted to cook great food."

"Isn't that the same thing?"

"Not really."

"So you split, and you came home. What happened to her?"

"She did great. Got what she wanted." He stared into the distance and Harry got the feeling he wasn't telling her the whole story. He might say he didn't want fame, but his look said otherwise.

"Are you still in touch?"

"Ah, no. For me, a split is a split."

"Of course," said Harry, and focused on the last of her stroganoff. A split is a split. A clear message from Jamie that she needed to keep her distance.

"YOU'VE GIVEN ME AN IDEA," Jamie said, as Harry scraped the last of the stroganoff from the bowl. "After the salmon incident, I started wondering if my recipe cards weren't clear. It got me thinking that maybe you'd be a good tester. Maybe you could cook some of my kits and I can watch how you interpret what I have in my head."

"You mean, if I can manage not to screw it up, anyone could cook it?"

Jamie grimaced.

"It's okay," Harry said. "I know where my talents lie and it's not in the kitchen."

Jamie raised an eyebrow, then lowered it again quickly. He could always turn a comment into a sexual innuendo, but that had been when he was a teenager.

Still, Harry laughed. "I'll be your guinea pig as long as you don't make me eat my burnt offerings."

"You won't ruin anything. I won't let it happen. Right then, Greek lamb kofta or creamy mustard chicken?"

"I just ate."

"Well then, you'll have to eat again."

"Then Greek," Harry said.

"All right," said Jamie. "Roll up your sleeves." He took a meal kit from the fridge and placed it in front of Harry. "I want you to make the meal as if I'm not here. Just follow the instructions so I can see exactly how you interpret them."

Harry looked skeptical, but he gave her an encouraging nod. She put on an apron and got to work.

Jamie watched Harry tear open the packets of herbs and tip them into the bowl of yogurt. She seemed nervous, and he smiled to himself at the idea of having a reputation as a hard-nosed chef. He wished she hadn't asked about the restaurant. Even now, it was still a sore spot for him. The failed business partnership had damaged his trust in others, and himself, and Jamie knew he needed to rebuild both if he was going to grow Local Goodness.

He glanced at his phone. Nothing from Ollie. That could mean the deliveries were going smoothly, or it could mean utter disaster. He put down the phone. He had to trust that Ollie could handle it.

"Okay," said Harry. She squinted at the card and placed a cucumber on the board.

Jamie brought his attention back to their work. "If you have a mandolin, you can slice these nice and thin in a jiffy," he told her.

"A what?"

"A slicer. You know." He made a motion as if running the cucumber over the sharp blade. "But if not, you can use a good old-fashioned knife."

He handed her a sharp knife, one he knew could turn the cucumbers into paper thin slivers. Harry gripped the knife in one hand and stretched her fingers down the length of the fruit. She lifted the knife.

"Wait!" he yelled. "Fingers definitely aren't in the recipe."

"I'm not planning to chop them off but I have to hold this thing or it will roll away."

"Can I show you?" he asked.

When Harry shrugged, he took her left hand and curled her fingers under so the tips of her nails rested on the cucumber's skin. "This way, if you slip, you won't lose a fingertip." He showed her how to hold the knife, encouraging her to relax her wrist.

Holding Harry's hand again after all these years sent a jolt of longing up his arm. Her slender fingers and delicate wrists were just as he remembered them. Her skin was as smooth as it had been back then, but it was a pampered smoothness now, softened with creams and lotions. She still kept her nails short and neat, but now manicured and painted with clean white tips instead of the purple glitter polish she'd worn the first time he had held her hand.

That day, they'd taken the train into town to see a movie about a boy from a mining town who dreamed of being a dancer. As they'd walked back to the station that evening, Harry talking about gender roles and old-fashioned beliefs, and how they had to be careful not to turn into their parents, Jamie had taken Harry's hand. The evening air had chilled her fingers, but heat radiated from her palm. He loved the feeling of their skin touching, of being connected to her at one simple point. In an easy, fluid motion, she had slipped each of her fingers in between his and squeezed, knitting the pair of them together. Forever, Jamie had thought in his boyish fantasy.

"Show me again," Harry said, pulling him back into the kitchen, back to the dangerously sharp knife that now hovered over her tender fingers.

Jamie blinked at the woman in his kitchen. He recalled the end of that date at the movies and, for a second, he pictured leaning in and kissing Harry again, tasting her lips, wondering how she might feel different from the Harry he had kissed back then, and how she might feel exactly the same.

"Jamie?" He snapped back to reality.

Harry peered at him, a worried look on her face. "Are you okay?"

He stared at her for a moment, then laughed. "I was just thinking about the two of us together."

"Good thoughts?"

"Very."

"We were pretty cute back then, weren't we?"

He straightened himself. *Get your act together, Forrest.* "Yes, we were. But that won't get you out of learning some knife skills. So..." He positioned Harry's hand on the knife. "Just relax. Don't force it. Let the motion be fluid and let the knife take the lead. Focus on the knife and the vegetable will do its thing."

Harry straightened her shoulders and closed her eyes. She took a breath, and Jamie thought she was going to say something more. Was she thinking about that first kiss, too? But then she shook out her wrist, gripped the knife, and sliced the cucumber into delicate slivers.

FOR THE BRIEFEST OF MOMENTS, Harry allowed herself to remember that first kiss. She was surprised Jamie had brought it up. Not the "steer clear" message she had picked up earlier. As he moved around the kitchen, his body floating with ease from one task to the next, she wondered what it would feel like now. She straightened her shoulders.

It was a pleasant memory of two people they'd once known. They were both changed now.

"I love watching you cook," she said. "You make me think of the sea lions at Pier 39 in San Francisco."

"Sea lions?"

"They're so awkward and lumbering on their little wooden rafts in the bay, and then they slip into the water and they're suddenly graceful and beautiful, like the water is the only place they're meant to be."

"I'm awkward and lumbering? Flattery will get you nowhere."

Harry laughed. "No. Definitely not. I just meant that when you're in the kitchen, you're different."

Truth be told, in the kitchen he moved like a dream. He carried himself with confidence, reaching for his tools and ingredients without looking. He mixed and stirred, holding up his end of a conversation while adding ingredients and tasting. "Like watching a ballet," she had told him when he'd cooked at Gran's. Likening his cooking to the grace and coordination of the dancers was a better comparison than the sea lions.

She'd been to the San Francisco Ballet with Tom once, and she'd cried when the handsome prince had kissed the sleeping princess and broken the fairy's evil spell. Tom had worn a tuxedo that night, and she'd worn a simple black dress with a plunging back. She remembered how he'd placed his hand on the lowest part of her back, his skin cool on hers, as he ushered her into their seventh-row seats. She remembered how artfully he'd removed that dress later in their hotel room. And she remembered how she'd woken the following morning to a note on his empty pillow, thanking her for a wonderful night. He'd left without even saying goodbye. She'd longed for the intimacy of waking up with him, to be with someone who stayed. She'd made excuses for Tom and his busy work schedule, and had blatantly ignored a niggling voice that said something wasn't right with their relationship. What had Jamie said to her about paying attention to the cooking? Keeping your focus on what was going on around you. All the signs of Tom's deceit had been right there in front of her; she'd just chosen to ignore them.

"You've really found your calling," Harry said. "It suits you."

"But I'm still the same old Jamie."

"Oh, you've changed," she said, thinking of the skinny teenage boy she'd loved and the man he'd become.

"Oh yeah? How so?"

Harry blushed. She'd been thinking about how Jamie had filled out, how his once-skinny arms were now muscled. "That's new, for one thing," she said, pointing to the tattoo on his arm. It was a sleeve of delicate vines winding around his arm. "What's the significance?"

"They're all my favorite herbs and botanicals," he said.

Harry leaned closer, picking out flowers and seeds, their Latin names inked alongside. The leaves and flowers curved and flexed with the muscles in his arm. Her face flushed hotter.

"Hey, Bossman," a voice called from the door. "I'm back."

Harry pulled away from Jamie's tattoo, her face flushing as if she'd been caught doing something she shouldn't.

"Ollie," Jamie said, running a hand through his hair, looking as flustered as she felt.

A tall, gangly blond man in thick Buddy Holly glasses ambled into the kitchen. He had the kind of baby face that made him look like a teenager, but Harry guessed he was in his early 20s. "Oh," he said, skidding to a halt when he saw Harry. "Didn't realize you had company, Bossman."

"I should get going," Harry said, suddenly wanting to get out of the stuffy kitchen. "It's getting late."

"It's four o'clock," Jamie said.

"I should check on Gran. And I have some things to do, and..." She took a breath, pulling herself together. "It was nice to meet you, Ollie. Great catching up, Jamie." She grabbed her phone and walked as calmly as her legs would allow to the door. "Thanks for lunch. And the lesson."

The lesson, she thought, as she hurried back across the road to Gran's, is that old flames don't always die out. But you can't go back in time. Not to someone whose heart you already broke.

CHAPTER SEVEN

GRAN'S OPERATION went without a hitch. When Harry saw her that evening, she was in good spirits, although a little woozy from the pain medication.

"We'll keep her in for a day or two to assess her progress," the nurse told Harry. "Once the incision heals nicely and your gran can get around with a walker, you can take her home."

"She's supposed to go to a wedding on Saturday," Harry said.

"It's possible," the nurse said, but from the way she scrunched up her face, Harry guessed it was unlikely. Still, if anyone could buck the odds, it was Gran.

"I'll be under your feet before you know it," Gran said, sleepily. "So you'd better have some fun for a couple of days. Let your hair down or something."

"Right," said Harry. "It'll be wild parties every night." More likely, she thought, it would be a job search. Next time Jamie asked about her life, she wanted to have something to tell him that at least looked like a plan. In the meantime, she would ignore the silly incident from earlier and keep her promise to help him with his recipes. At the very least, it meant she wouldn't have cereal for dinner and she wouldn't have to eat alone.

Sitting down to eat with someone every night had made Harry realize how often she ate alone in San Francisco. Breakfast was often a protein shake on her morning commute (not exactly eating alone as she often sipped her smoothies crammed into MUNI.) Lunch might be a salad picked up from the vendor in the lobby and eaten at her desk. She attempted to have a healthy dinner, stopping for takeout from one of the growing number of farm-to-table spots in her neighborhood, or heating one of the overpriced prepared meals she had delivered every couple of weeks. Sometimes she'd go to her favorite local restaurant, Giovanni's, just so she could chat to the owner while she ate his delicious grilled sardines. But many times she had eaten granola and yogurt alone in her PJs, too exhausted to bother with proper food. Or maybe too alone.

Cooking and eating with Jamie would mean nutritious food and charming company. She was looking forward to both.

Back at the house, Harry unpacked Jamie's Chicken Marsala to cook herself a healthy dinner and keep her promise to test his meal kits. She studied the instructions, following Jamie's advice to read them all the way through first, to avoid surprises, and then laying out all the ingredients before she started cooking.

"*Mise en place*," she said to herself in a poor French accent.

"Get your act together first," is how Jamie had explained it.

She found a set of small bowls in Gran's cupboard and was just snipping the corner of the packet of Cremini mushrooms when her phone rang. When Harry saw it was Soraya, she took the call.

"Harry! How're you surviving in the sticks, girlfriend? Making your own moonshine yet?" Soraya laughed, that deep, rumbling laugh of hers.

"Chicken Marsala, actually."

"You are too funny. How's your gran?"

"Doing great."

"Oh, good. Now, you haven't run into any old flames and had a rebound fling, have you?"

"No." Harry twisted the vowel in a way that made her sound guilty. Fortunately, Soraya missed it.

"Listen. I'm working on the last details for the girls' weekend."

"Great," Harry said. Soraya, Harry, and two of their friends had been talking about a girls' weekend away for weeks now. Soraya wanted to go to Vegas, Harry suggested Tahoe, Leilani insisted on going to the coast, and Jessenia thought they should do Disneyland.

"When're you back?" Soraya asked.

Harry tucked the phone under her chin and snipped open a bag of parsley. "End of the month," Harry said, thinking how nice it would be to have a girls' trip to look forward to. "Did you book something?"

"Not yet," said Soraya. "Waiting on you."

Harry thought about the weeks ahead. With luck, she'd have interviews lined up, maybe even a job to go back to. She had told no one yet that she might move east. If she was smart, she'd leave her calendar open.

"You know, things are a little uncertain here, with my gran and all. If you find a weekend that works for the others, book it."

"And go without you?"

Harry's stomach twisted. This was always the hardest part of moving on, leaving behind people she'd grown attached to. "Book it anyway and we'll figure it out."

"Okay," Soraya said. "If you're sure."

Harry wasn't sure. "I'm sure."

"What's that noise?" Soraya asked. "Like something rustling."

"I told you, I'm cooking," Harry said. "Chicken Marsala."

"You're cooking?" Soraya said, with the same disdain Harry would have expected if she'd said she was eating small children. "Well, aren't you domesticated."

"It's relaxing," Harry said, and realized it was true. She'd always hated cooking, getting anxious about trying to do all the right steps at the right time. But cooking with Jamie wasn't like that at all. It felt comfortable, normal, something couples did together all the time.

"You definitely need to get your butt back here soon, girl, because I don't think I know you anymore."

Harry put down the chicken she had just dredged in flour. Comfortable? Couples? What on earth was her mind twittering on about? Soraya was right. She needed to find a job and get back to work, back to her normal life. Cooking was a pleasant distraction, but she couldn't support herself without a job.

She put the meal kit back in the fridge and poured herself a bowl of Gran's muesli and a large glass of wine. Then she set up her laptop at the kitchen table and got busy looking for a job.

There was no shortage of opportunities for Harry. She could probably find work anywhere in the world, if that's what she wanted, as long as she could get Spike past customs. As she searched, a job in London popped up. She had all the qualifications and the salary was good. Plus it offered remote work with monthly trips into the city. If she lived here, it would be ideal. But she didn't live here. She clicked away and focused on jobs in the U.S. Within the hour, she had her resume in inboxes at six firms in three cities. One of them would call. She was back on track.

Harry was having another go at the Chicken Marsala when she heard a knock at the door. It was just after eight, not late, but in the city, no one showed up uninvited after dark. Harry wondered if she should call the police. She grabbed her phone and tiptoed to the backdoor. She flicked on the porch light and came eye to eye with a face, peering through the patterned glass panel. A woman's face, as far as she could tell.

"Harry?" She didn't recognize the voice. "It's me. Sarah. I'm just checking on your gran."

Harry frowned. The woman sounded friendly, but if her intentions were truly good, why not just use the phone? Harry wedged her foot behind the door and opened it just enough to peek out. On the doorstep was a woman about her own age. She wore khaki short overalls and Wellington boots, her long, buttery-yellow hair hanging in two messy braids over her shoulders. She beamed at Harry like they were old friends.

"Sorry to come so late, but I saw your light was on and I thought I'd pop in. How's your gran?"

Harry hesitated. "I saw her tonight. She's doing okay."

The woman clutched the neck of her thin t-shirt. "I'm so glad. Your gran is such a treasure. You must be relieved."

"I am," Harry said. "Um, I'm don't mean to be rude, but I don't think we've met, have we?"

"Oh my goodness, no. I'm so sorry. I'm Sarah. Michael's

partner. Wife-to-be, I think I can say now." She giggled. "Must get used to that."

Harry had no idea who Michael was. Then it all clicked into place. "Oh, Sarah. You're the one getting married on Saturday."

"That's me."

"Come in," Harry said, and opened the door.

Sarah grinned and thrust a small box of snap peas into Harry's hand. "First ones of the season. Thought you might enjoy them. Oh, I brought some more honey for your gran." She handed Harry a jar.

"Thanks," said Harry, still a little taken aback by the whirlwind in her kitchen. "Would you like some tea or something?"

"I'd love to, but I can't stay. Got tons to do before Saturday. I'm not usually this scatterbrained. Honest." She gave a laugh that seemed to squeeze in her throat, and Harry suspected that, if Sarah made it to the wedding without having a complete meltdown, she was going to sleep through the entire honeymoon. "Now, I wanted to ask you... I didn't realize you'd be here until Jamie mentioned it to Michael, but we'd love you to come on Saturday. You can be your gran's plus one."

Harry didn't answer at first. She was still picturing Jamie telling his oldest and best friend about her and wondering what he'd said. And then she was picturing Michael, who she'd known as a teenager, and wondering what he looked like now. And didn't he have a sister? Or maybe two?

"I don't have clothes for a wedding," Harry said, her mind quickly scrambling to think of something she could say in response to Sarah.

Sarah laughed. "Oh, don't worry about that. It's really

casual. I made my dress. And Jamie's serving lunch at hay-bale tables. It will all be very low key. Will you come? It'll be fun."

According to Jamie, Sarah and Michael had a small farm at the end of the village that they had turned into a thriving homestead. They fed themselves on their produce, supplied Michael's sister's B&B, and provided several ingredients to Local Goodness. Sarah had installed beehives the previous spring, and this year had harvested sufficient honey to sell. Jamie was already experimenting with recipes that could use Sarah's honey. If Sarah said it was going to be a casual affair, she probably meant it.

"If you're sure it's no trouble," Harry said.

"I'd love to have you. You'll probably know half the people, anyway." She threw her arms around Harry and pulled her into a long hug. "Any friend of Jamie's is a friend of Michael's. And any friend of Michael's is a friend of mine." And with that, she left.

When Harry went to bed that night, she slept a long and restful sleep. Gran was going to be fine, Harry had feelers out for a job, and now she had a new friend in Hope.

JAMIE BLINKED at the man sitting across the small wooden table at The Cat's Whiskers tea room.

"I have a physics degree," the man was saying, "and a clean driver's license. It's all in my application."

A pressed shirt strained across the solid mass of the man's body, which was crammed onto a frail-looking wooden chair. The late morning sun shining through the tea room window bounced off the shiny dome of the man's shaved head. When he picked up the delicate china cup and saucer to sip his Earl Grey tea, Jamie spotted tattoos across both knuckles. He wasn't sure whether to offer the man a shortbread or just hand over his homework and lunch money.

"You're a bit over-qualified," Jamie said, glancing over the man's application. Terrence, the form said. "Just Terry," the man had said. Terry did in fact have a physics degree, which Jamie supposed would come in handy for balancing stacks of meal kit boxes. But when Jamie pictured this brick wall of a man filling the doorways of his customer's homes, he wondered if he might not be a tad intimidating.

"I work at the university in town," Terry said, pointing again to his application. "But my mam's not been well and I'm looking for something closer to home. We live just over the hill."

"Oh," Jamie said. "I'm sorry to hear about your mother."

"She's doing a lot better now. But she's not getting any younger. I thought this job would be ideal, as I could check in on her on my rounds. On my break, of course. I wouldn't be taking work time or anything. But I could stop in, make her a quick cup of tea, keep an eye on her." His face broke into a gentle smile that made him look like an over-sized teddy-bear. "You know how we blokes are with our mams." He laughed and braided his tattooed fingers across his belly so that Jamie could read them. "Mam" was written across one hand, and "Dad" across the other. When Jamie had decided on his own tattoo, he'd thought carefully about what was important to him, what he cared most about. He couldn't help but think that this gentle giant could end up being a hit with some of his older customers.

"I've a few more interviews to do, but I'll be in touch," Jamie said. He tried to sound encouraging without giving false hope.

Terry's face fell, but he snatched it back into a smile. "Appreciate your time," he said and shook Jamie's hand.

Jamie watched him lumber down the street to a newer model silver sedan. He climbed in, put on his seatbelt, flipped on his turn signal, and checked before pulling away from the curb. All very safe and conservative, if only Jamie would give him a chance.

As he waited for his next candidate, Britni, to arrive, Jamie stared out the window of The Cat's Whiskers, his gaze resting on Mrs. Belmont's cottage. He wondered what Harry was doing now.

It had been fun to catch up with her yesterday. Just like old times. When they'd been an item, they had talked endlessly, both of them comfortable being honest and open. Even when Harry had dumped him, she'd been upfront about her reasons. "We both need to be free to follow our dreams," she'd said, and he'd trusted her reasoning, even if he hadn't liked it.

But last night, she'd been cagey. When he'd pressed her to talk about whatever was so obviously on her mind, she'd dodged his question and turned it back on him. Of course, he hadn't been exactly forthright either. He'd done a fine tap-dance around the failure of Slate, and he'd dodged entirely any details about Alexis. But that was ancient history, and he had no use for digging up the past. He had to focus on the future.

He couldn't stop thinking about the idea of opening a restaurant again. Just his, no entanglement with business partners. But the last thing he needed now was to take on a new venture when he was struggling to manage Local Goodness. Still, it never hurt to dream a little.

While he waited for his next interviewee, he called the number he'd scribbled on the back of his application folder that morning, and spoke to a man named Cameron McKenzie. By the time Britni arrived, ten minutes late and looking like she was still wearing pajamas, Jamie had a meeting with Cameron arranged for that evening. His date with destiny. He wasn't sure whether to be excited or terrified. He opted for both.

MICHAEL WAS ALREADY at their usual table at The Butcher's Arms when Jamie arrived.

"All ready for the Big Day?" Jamie asked.

Michael grinned. "Ready, willing, and able, my friend." He took a slug of his beer and gave Michael a wry look. "And how was your afternoon with Harry Belmont?"

"No idea what you're talking about."

"I'm outside all day. I see everything." He grinned.

Jamie waved him off. "She was worried about her gran and all that."

"And so she turned to you. Makes perfect sense."

Jamie focused on the foam on the top of his pint and tried to push away thoughts of Harry at his kitchen table. He had a sudden memory of Harry in the mornings. When they were a couple, Harry always looked her best first thing in the morning. When most people woke up with wild hair, skin like bread dough, and breath like rotting vegetables, Harry always looked the way she did in Jamie's dreams, fuzzy around the edges, but serene and beautiful.

"Oh, bloody hell," said Jamie.

"She's still under your skin, isn't she?"

"Bloody, bloody hell."

"Maybe that's why you've tried and failed abysmally to find someone else. You've never given up on Harry."

Jamie shook his head. "It's not that. She's lit a fire under me again, like she always did."

"I bet she has."

"Not like that. Well, a bit like that. She's got me thinking about what I really want."

"Which is?"

Jamie thought about cooking, about what it would be like to have his own restaurant on his terms. His mind tumbled with all the ways his business could grow, how he could follow his dreams again. And mixed up in all of it was Harry.

"I think you need another beer," Jamie said.

"My round," Michael said, and pushed up to go to the bar.

Left alone, Jamie's thoughts ran straight to Harry. He wanted to tell Michael about the ideas she'd sparked in him when they'd cooked together. His fantasies were suddenly filled again with restaurant concepts, a twist on his delivery business, the foodie columns raving about him leading the pack in farm-to-table innovation. Harry had done that, just like she always had.

"Tourist alert," Michael said as he slipped back into his seat. "I think this guy walked into the wrong pub."

Jamie twisted his neck to see a dark-haired man surveying the pub. He wore a green Barbour jacket, perfect for the country, but his jeans were designer, his shirt tailored, and his brown leather boots spotless. Even his dog looked like an accessory he'd picked out for his country look. "Ah, I think this is my date."

Before Michael could put his dropped jaw into action to ask what on earth he was talking about, Jamie was up and waving the man over.

"Jamie?" the man asked.

Jamie shook the man's hand and patted the dog's head. The dog immediately leaned on his leg as if he'd found a new best friend.

"Cameron McKenzie," the man said. "And this is Baxter."

"Get you a beer?"

"I can't stay, I'm afraid. Sorry. Got another appointment a half hour from here." He handed Jamie a brown envelope. "I'm staying in the area for the night, so maybe I can pass back through after lunch tomorrow and we can talk?"

"Sounds great," said Jamie, his heart thudding.

"It has a lot of potential, but you'll have to use your imagination for now."

Jamie nodded. He could do that.

"And watch your step," Cameron added.

"What was that?" Michael said after Cameron and Baxter had left.

Jamie grinned. "That, my friend, was my future."

CHAPTER NINE

EARLY THE NEXT MORNING, Jamie called Harry. "Do you have a few minutes? I'd like your opinion on something."

Twenty minutes later, they stood outside the old village shop. Harry looked tired.

"I spoke to Gran this morning. She's in a lot of pain," she said.

"You should have said. Can I take you over to visit? This can wait." He had a million things to do before the wedding, but he couldn't leave Harry alone when she was clearly worried.

"I'll go this afternoon. She'll be okay. Just perhaps not as resilient as I thought." She forced a smile.

Jamie had the urge to wrap his arms around her and tell her it would be okay. Instead, he squeezed her shoulder. "She's tough, your gran."

"I know." She frowned at the boarded-up windows and peeling door of the village shop. "So, what's this opinion you're after?"

Jamie calmed his nerves. "Okay, so I've been thinking

about what you said about the restaurant. And you're right. I'm really proud of Local Goodness, and it's doing well. Too well. But I'm hiding behind it so I don't have to step out there and do what I really want to do."

"Which is?"

"I want to cook again, open a restaurant. Not in London. Not with a partner. Not with a high concept designed to take the culinary world by storm. I want an intimate little bistro with a few tables that fill every night. I want to run a place where I can step out of the kitchen and talk to my patrons, where people can feel like they're coming home for dinner."

Harry smiled. "Sounds amazing."

"This place came up and—keep your mind open—I think it's got potential."

He turned the key in the lock and pushed open the dusty door, its window thick with cobwebs. The electricity was off, but he left the door open to let in some light and lit his camping lamp so they could see the space.

Debris left by the previous owners covered the old stone floor: chipped metal shelving screwed to the worn oak beams, battered boxes left behind, a price tag, tattered posters advertising local events long since forgotten. Against one wall was a stack of wood. Jamie worried someone had removed it from an important structural element. A thick layer of dust covered everything, and the musky tang of furry residents hung in the air.

"You'll have to use your imagination," Jamie said, repeating Cameron's words and hoping she wouldn't need too much imagination.

Harry stepped inside, deftly avoiding a pile of debris. With the toe of her shoe, she scraped across the dusty floor and peered down at the stone flags beneath. She ran a hand over one of the exposed oak beams. Jamie's heart sank. The place was a dump, almost ready to fall down. His gut had warned him, and now Harry was confirming his fears.

"There's a sizable room through here," he said, leading her through an archway. He felt like a little boy showing a new friend his room and trying to impress her with a new toy he could suddenly see was disappointing. "I think it was a storage room, but if I took out the shelves, maybe there'd be room for a working kitchen." His voice trailed off.

Harry's gaze skipped around the room as if she were taking in every detail. "What's through here?" she asked, reaching for the back door.

"It's a mess," he said, taking the key from the ring Cameron McKenzie had given him, and unlocking the back door. "It might have been a garden once, but it's suffered some serious neglect." He opened the door to show Harry the three-foot tall grass, the dilapidated fence wound with brambles, and the ramshackle outbuilding that looked as if it might fall down in the first stiff breeze.

Harry gasped.

"I know," Jamie said. "It's pretty bad..."

"It's perfect."

"I think you need glasses."

"It's just how I imagined it."

Jamie didn't understand at first that Harry had imagined a place for him at all, and second that she'd imagine a dump like this.

"This is your patio," Harry said, sweeping her hand across the expanse of nettles and brambles. "You can use that building to frame it, build a pergola from the wood in there. Match the stone, add some simple decor and lighting, and this could be really cozy. And you could double your capacity."

"This is England. We'd be able to use this about three days a year."

"So you build an outdoor fireplace or put in heaters, enclose it to protect it from the weather. You could put in some raised beds and grow herbs for the kitchen, sort of merge the patio and garden. People would love that."

Now that Jamie looked again at the weeds and exposed brick, he could see what Harry saw. He pictured his guests eating out here under a ceiling of twinkly lights while he circulated among the tables. "What about the inside?"

Harry's face lit up, and she hurried back indoors. "This stone floor is amazing. I bet once it's cleaned up it will be gorgeous. You could go with a rustic feel. Expose those oak beams, clean up the floor. Go with simple wood tables, bold country-style dishes, maybe a single stem gerbera in a simple vase on each table. If you had a fireplace in here..."

Jamie didn't dare interrupt her as she looked around. He could almost see her mind turning a mile a minute as she planned out his dream restaurant.

And in that moment, Jamie had a vision of his own. He pictured Harry greeting guests inside the big wooden door, explaining the menu and the concept of his restaurant. He pictured sitting at one of the simple wooden tables with her, planning out the season's menu. And he pictured locking up the restaurant after hours and walking home through the quiet streets of the village with Harry beside him.

"Oh, my God!" Harry shouted.

Jamie snapped back into the room. Harry was balancing on a pile of rubble in a gap between two shelving racks. With a broken paint stirrer in her hand, she was poking behind a board that was screwed to the wall. One corner popped away and Harry jimmied the other with the stick. As Jamie stepped around a crushed cardboard box, trying to see what Harry had found, and hoping it wasn't anything gruesome that would shut the restaurant before it had even opened, the board sprung from the wall. Behind it was an enormous stone fireplace sunk deep into the wall. The hearth had blackened from years, possibly centuries, of use. To one side was a nook with a stone shelf that bore the ring marks of heavy cooking pots. A hole in the back opened to a stone bread oven, the likes of which Jamie had only ever seen in pictures. On the other side was a rusting black box that Jamie knew would clean up to be a black lead stove. The whole thing took up enough space for at least two more tables.

He suspected the previous shop owners had failed to get planning permission to take it out—probably because the building was so old—so had boarded it up instead. "Oh great," he said.

"It is great," said Harry. "It's perfect." She beamed at him and her eyes lit up like it was Christmas morning. She stepped down from the pile of rubble and, before Jamie knew what was happening, she wrapped her arms around his neck and kissed him. "It's just how I imagined it."

"You imagined it?"

"The whole thing. When I thought about a restaurant of your design, this is exactly what I saw—the stone floors, the oak beams, the patio out back, even this." She gestured toward the fireplace. "This is it. It's home."

Jamie smiled, seeing the rundown dump of a place through Harry's eyes. She was right. When he thought about creating simple food with local ingredients, sharing it with customers who knew him by first name, people who came back week after week for the comfort of his cooking, this is just what he had in mind. "Home," he said. "That would be the perfect name."

"Welcome home," Harry said and hugged him again.

With Harry's head pressed against his shoulder, Jamie surveyed the old shop again. It was perfect. And standing here with Harry Belmont in his arms again felt like exactly where he wanted to be. Home.

CHAPTER TEN

GRAN WAS SLEEPING when Harry went to see her at the hospital that afternoon. She had some swelling, the nurse told Harry, and they were keeping an eye on her. Harry sat by her bedside, watching her sleep. The longer Gran stayed in the hospital, the more worried Harry became that she might not bounce back. Her gran was resilient, but that didn't mean she was invincible. If Harry had to change her plans and stay longer to help Gran, she would. It wasn't like she had anywhere to be yet, anyway.

When Jamie insisted on driving her to the hospital to visit Gran the next day, Harry almost sighed with relief.

"I'm going into town, anyway," he told her. "I have some last-minute things to pick up for the wedding."

Harry accepted, grateful for his upbeat company.

Jamie chattered the entire way into town, talking about the restaurant and ideas that had come to him in the night. His excitement filled the cab of his van, and Harry couldn't help but notice how alive he had become. He had misgivings, which Harry thought was normal for a new venture, and a good sign. But the excitement radiating from him told her he was making the right decision. This was what he was destined to do.

When Harry arrived at the hospital, she was shocked to see Gran sitting up in bed, while a nurse helped situate her on a walker.

"Can you believe these sadists are making me walk?" Gran said.

The nurse only laughed. "Best thing for you, Mrs. Belmont," she said.

"How are you feeling?" Harry asked as she and Gran began a slow shuffle down the ward.

"As long as they keep giving me these painkillers, I'll be great." Gran laughed.

"You can't take them forever. You know that, don't you?"

"Don't worry. I won't become an addict. But while they're being offered, I may as well. It's been a long time since I've woken up without everything hurting. I'm ready to wake up in my own bed again, though."

"I don't think they're going to release you quite yet, Gran," Harry said, steadying her grandmother.

"Once I can make it to the end of the ward on my own, they'll let me go." Gran leaned on her walker and winced. "I don't think it's going to be today, though. Looks like I'll miss the wedding."

"Sarah invited me. Last minute," Harry said. "I could take pictures for you. It won't be the same, but at least you can feel you were there."

Gran's face lit up. "I want to see her dress. And get pictures of Michael all dressed up. He was always a handsome boy. And his niece is a bridesmaid, I think."

Harry smiled. "I'll get pictures of everything, including the cake."

"Have you seen much of Jamie while I've been in here?"

"What?" Harry asked, her face flushing hot.

"I imagine you two had a lot of catching up to do," Gran said, with a wry smile.

Harry looked at Gran and tried to keep her expression from betraying her. "We've been talking. You know Jamie."

"Jamie?" A familiar voice crept into Harry's ear. From behind an enormous bouquet of funereal lilies, Barbara smiled.

"Mum? What are you doing here?"

"I came to see my mother." She leaned in and kissed Gran on each cheek.

"I think that's enough exercise for me for today," Gran said, and turned in a slow circle back to her bed.

"What a bonus to see you, too," Barbara said, kissing Harry.

In spite of herself, Harry smiled. Her mother could be flighty and completely self-involved, but when she turned her attention on you, it was intoxicating. Still, Harry hurried to catch Gran and help her back to bed.

"You're not talking about little Jamie Forrest, are you?" Barbara asked, striding beside them. "Oh, you two were so sweet together. Still, that's all in the past. How's Tom?"

Gran shot Harry a sideways look, but Harry said nothing. She couldn't even remember mentioning Tom to Barbara, and even if she had, she'd doubted Barbara would have listened. But apparently she had.

"You broke up," Barbara said, when Harry didn't answer. She shook her head. "You career girls never want to settle, do you?"

"You want a coffee, Mum? I was just going to get one."

Barbara waved her off. "I can't stay long."

"Then I'll give you two some time alone," Harry said, and went to find the cafeteria.

She needed to cool off before she said something to her mother she'd later regret. Her mother could push her buttons, as if provoking Harry into a childish outburst would somehow cement Barbara's position as the mother figure. Harry sometimes felt that Barbara was in a constant battle to keep her daughter down, whereas Gran had done everything in her power to build Harry up and encourage her to fly. And even though it had meant Harry had flown far away, Gran had never held it against her. Ironically, Gran's lack of pressure and guilt made Harry wish she was closer now. Harry didn't regret moving halfway around the world, but she wished it was easier to see Gran more often. She had to admit that the mess with Tom and losing her job had a bright silver lining. Harry was glad she could be here for Gran to make up in a small way for all the times she'd been absent. She wondered if Barbara felt the same, that perhaps she had finally grown to appreciate her mother.

But when she got back to Gran's room, all that remained of Barbara was the pungent smell of lilies, only slightly over-powered by too much expensive perfume.

"Well, that was nice," Gran said, without a hint of sarcasm.

"She came all this way to spend five minutes with you?"

"Of course not," Gran said. "She came for the wedding."

Harry's stomach fell. She'd been looking forward to the wedding. It would be good to get out and let her hair down a bit and, of course, Jamie would be there. But Barbara's pres-ence would change everything. Harry could never relax with her around.

"How did she get an invitation?"

"Oh, she's known Michael's mother for donkey's years. You know your mum, never one to miss a party."

"I know," said Harry.

"But that mustn't stop you going and enjoying yourself." Harry shrugged. It would.

"No, Harry," Gran said. "You walk in there like you own the place. You get on the dance floor, you enjoy yourself. Meet some people your own age. It's time you made some friends."

"I have friends at home," Harry said. "I'm not staying, remember?"

"I know," said Gran. "But it will be good to go, let your hair down, dance with a stranger. That's what weddings are for. That's how I ended up with your grandfather."

"Really?"

"His brother was the best man at my friend's sister's wedding. I danced by myself all night, which wasn't done in those days. And I could see him watching me, but he never plucked up the courage to ask me to dance. Silly sod. Finally, it was the second to last song, and I thought, 'Right, that's it.' I marched over and pulled him on to the dance floor before he could object. Bit forward of me, but I told him, 'When you see something you want, you have to go for it.'"

Harry laughed. She had no trouble picturing Gran on the dance floor, catching the eye of the handsome young man who would become Harry's grandfather. It was impossibly romantic.

"I'll go," Harry said. "But I assure you I won't be picking up any strange men."

Harry smiled all the way home, thinking about Gran on that dance floor. She wondered how she would have turned out if she hadn't had Gran's influence. Maybe she would never have had the courage to leave Hope, or maybe she would have trailed around after her mother until she was flung off into her own ungrounded orbit.

When Jamie dropped her off, she thanked him for taking her and said she looked forward to seeing him at the wedding. When she checked her email after lunch, there was a response from the company in Boston, requesting an interview for the following Monday. Harry responded immediately and accepted the invitation. Boston would be perfect. A brand new chapter in her life and a four-hour shorter flight time for when she wanted to visit Gran. She promised herself she would visit more often once she moved.

But as she closed down her laptop, a little knot twinged in her insides. She knew she would have to leave Gran in a couple of weeks. She had a life elsewhere waiting for her. But the possibility of a job in Boston made it real, and suddenly she wasn't ready to leave. She wanted more time to get Gran up to full capacity again, more time to explore Hope and get to know Sarah. She would love to watch Jamie follow his dreams and open Home, too.

But seeing her mother reminded Harry that she didn't belong here. If she wanted to continue to bloom, she had to plant herself in more fertile soil. With luck, that soil would be in Boston.

CHAPTER ELEVEN

____

ON SATURDAY MORNING, Harry stepped through a gate into the field behind Michael and Sarah's farm. The sun shone in a clear blue sky, and the scent of fresh flowers wrapped around her. Bales of hay stood in rows, draped with garlands of wildflowers and capped at the ends with sprays of lilacs. The event had a lively air that was a far cry from the few formal church ceremonies Harry recalled attending when she lived here. Music drifted over from a band in the corner, but instead of the hymns and classical pieces Harry had expected, two men with hip beards and skinny suits and a woman in a 1940s dress and rolled hair played covers of romantic classics.

"Bride or groom?" asked a man, handing her a paper program and a cone of rose petals.

Harry hesitated. She'd only met Sarah once, and she hadn't seen Michael since they were teenagers. "Bride," she said, deciding that Sarah had invited her, and as she wasn't from Hope, she would probably have fewer guests.

The usher pointed her to the far side of the field, where she immediately spotted Jamie standing with the groom.

They both wore the same pale lemon shirts and neatly pressed gray trousers, but Harry's eyes zipped right to Jamie and the way the afternoon sun caught the chestnut highlights in his neatly cropped hair. He turned as if sensing Harry's presence and his eyes lit up along with a bright, welcoming smile. Harry's insides fluttered and something in her chest gave an unexpected ping. Jamie whispered something to Michael and hurried over.

"You came," he said.

"I promised Gran lots of photos." A fresh, clean scent drifted to Harry's nose. Jamie had undone the top two buttons of his shirt so that the collar fell open, revealing a triangle of freshly scrubbed skin. Harry smiled to herself at how nicely Jamie cleaned up. "You're best man *and* caterer?"

Jamie grinned so that all three dimples on one side of his mouth curled in. "I'm a man of many talents."

Harry's face went warm, but she gave him a serious smile. "I know."

"You look lovely, by the way."

Harry didn't admit that she'd spent hours Googling country weddings to gauge appropriate attire for guests. Her findings had ranged from tailored dresses and elaborate fascinators to strappy sundresses and wellies. In the end, she'd taken Sarah's assurance that the event was informal, and opted for a dress she'd packed as an afterthought—pale peach printed with gray and white flowers. The boat neck and capped sleeves were demure enough that they wouldn't draw attention away from the bride, but the form-fitting line and above-the-knees hemline gave it a flirty playfulness that might be noticed by the best man.

He noticed. Jamie's eyes swept down her, taking in

every detail, yet never lingering long enough to make her uncomfortable.

"You look lovely, too," Harry said. She was about to say more when a ripple passed thorough the congregation. She turned, expecting to see the bride, but instead her mother swanned down the aisle as if she were the star attraction. Harry tried to make herself invisible, hoping she'd been away so long that people wouldn't remember they were related.

No such luck. Barbara spotted Harry, wiggled her fingers and glided over, Graham in tow.

Harry actually liked her mother's husband, although she never saw much of him. He'd rarely accompanied Barbara on the few times she'd visited Gran and Harry. They came together once to bring a gift for Harry's 16th birthday, and again to announce they were married. After Harry moved away, she'd seen Graham at her university graduation, and again when he and Barbara were passing through San Diego on a cruise from Florida to Alaska via the Panama Canal. Graham had been pleasant and chatty, asking Harry questions that prompted interesting discussions, which Barbara ultimately turned back toward herself.

He stepped past Barbara now and squeezed Harry's shoulders, pecking her on one cheek. "Harry," he said. He reached across her and shook Jamie's hand as if Jamie were her date. "Graham Townsend," he said. "Glad to meet you."

"Oh, he's not...," Harry began, but Jamie interrupted.

"Jamie Forrest."

"Ah, you're the chap who owns that terrific food service operation, aren't you?"

"Local Goodness. Guilty as charged."

Graham slipped a business card from his jacket pocket

with a practiced move. "If you ever expand into London, give me a call. You'd be a hit there, I can tell you."

"Oh, Gray, must you always talk business?" Barbara said, pride oozing between her words.

Just then, the band launched into a rendition of a song Harry vaguely remembered from her childhood. "That's my cue," Jamie said, and hurried back to Michael.

Just before he was out of earshot, Barbara gave Harry a sly smirk. "Looks like someone's still carrying a torch for you," she whispered, and ushered Graham onto a hay-bale pew, laying down a silk scarf before she sat.

Harry sighed. Leave it to Barbara to see something that wasn't there. But when she turned to where Jamie had gone, he glanced over his shoulder and grinned. Just under the knot in the belt at Harry's waist, something tickled. She looked away and hurried to her seat next to her mother.

After a pair of little girls in simple cotton dresses and adorable pink wellington boots had scattered petals down the aisle, the band switched to *"The Pushbike Song"* and the bride appeared from behind a chicken coop. Harry lifted her phone to capture pictures of Sarah's homemade dress. Gran would be thrilled. The dress was simple and flowing, soft ivory fabric with antique lace at the shoulders and an empire waist, the skirt flowing in a single layer of sheer fabric, embellished with a wide lace band. The bride wore her sun-kissed hair loose, caught up at the sides and held with a simple wreath of flowers. She wore barely any make-up, but her skin glowed with the radiance of someone who spent time outdoors. To Harry, she was absolutely lovely.

At the altar, Michael beamed like he'd just taken first prize at the village fair, and Harry's throat tightened. It was so clear these two adored one another, and Harry wondered how it would be to have someone look at her that way. She thought about Tom—Tom and Meredith, Tom and Harry, Tom and who knows who else. What a joke. Something bubbled in the rims of her eyes and she blinked back tears.

When her vision cleared again, Jamie was looking right at her. Was she imagining it, or did he just wink? She smiled back at him, and a giddiness wriggled through her as the warmth of Jamie's smile wrapped around her and squeezed.

At her side, Barbara glanced at Harry. "Don't let your roots take hold, Harry," Barbara whispered, "or you'll end up here forever."

Harry kept her eyes forward. The tingle of Jamie's smile faded, and she tried to grab hold of it. She focused on the wedding, the joy of this couple cementing their love. But all she could think about now was if it would ever happen for her. Somehow it seemed unlikely.

~

IT WAS ALREADY hot in the marquee, but Jamie remained remarkably cool. After the ceremony—which was flawless—he'd changed out of his best man's shirt and trousers, and slipped into jeans and a chef coat. He was immediately at home.

A young server bustled through the marquee entrance. "What's next, Chef?"

Jamie loved the sound of that title. He allowed himself a moment to glow, then pointed to a plate of hors d'oeuvres. "Smoked salmon toast points. Sausage rolls coming next."

The server took the plate and hurried out. Jamie strode across to another table where another server was arranging salads on a plate. "Don't overdo the dressing. They can ask for more, but you don't want it swimming."

Sarah and Michael had insisted it be a casual affair, but

Jamie wanted everything to be perfect for his friends' big day. He slid back to the entrance to check on the lunch. The guests were mingling, taking nibbles from the server's plates. Everyone looked content. Good.

He spotted Michael talking to Sarah's friend. Carmen, was it? Michael had introduced them earlier, and she seemed nice enough. Jamie had promised his friend he would seek her out later. And then he spotted Harry. She was talking to Michael's sister Kate and her partner. Harry looked lovely with the afternoon sun glinting off her hair, and her body slipped into a peach and gray dress. He willed her to notice him.

"The food's amazing. Oh my God." Jamie snapped out of his Harry moment to find Michael's other sister, Nicki, beaming at him from outside the tent. "Michael says you're considering a restaurant? I would love that. I'm always grumbling about having to send guests out of the village for a posh dinner. I could send you people every day."

Nicki ran Sunnydale, the cozy bed-and-breakfast in the village. Jamie could imagine a steady stream of her guests coming to his restaurant. In his wildest fantasies, the owners of B&Bs in other villages would send their guests, too. But at that moment, his mind was on Harry.

"You should go for it," Nicki said.

"I'm still running some numbers, but—"

"I don't just mean the restaurant."

Jamie glanced at Nicki. She gave him a sneaky smile. He'd been staring at Harry, and she knew it. "Yeah, well, I think that bird flew the coop a long time ago."

"And yet, here she is, come home to roost."

Jamie laughed. "Have you talked to her? I assure you, she is not settling back in here, if that's what you're thinking."

"And yet, she dropped everything to be here for her grandmother."

"As anyone would."

"And I saw how she looked at those cute little bridesmaids. Trust me when I tell you, she may have flown the coop, but she's come home to nest."

Jamie stared across the field. He pictured Harry in his kitchen, Harry with her gran. Harry with his children. He shook his head to clear his thoughts. Nicki had it all wrong. Harry had made it quite clear this was a temporary stay.

And then Harry flicked her head back to laugh at something Kate had said. When she looked back, she stared right at him. Her face dropped from the laugh into a gentle smile, a smile that spread across her whole face, all the way to her eyes. Underneath his chef coat, just under his embroidered name, Jamie's heart did a little flip.

THE WEDDING LUNCH was served in a small orchard, where six long tables and bench sets had been constructed from hay bales. They were decorated with mismatched tableware, colorful plates, and glasses of every shape. Paper bunting draped between the trees and fluttered in the faint afternoon breeze.

All through lunch, Barbara circulated the tables, greeting old friends and making new ones while Graham talked Harry's ear off about business. He didn't ask once about her life—or Gran—but Harry was grateful not to have to make conversation. Instead, she just enjoyed Jamie's food.

Before dessert was served, Barbara made her last good-byes and told Harry they were leaving. "It's a long drive back and Graham doesn't know anyone here."

Harry couldn't help but notice how her mother looked longingly at the place beyond the trees where the band—now six musicians—was setting up beside a temporary plywood dance floor for the evening festivities. But Graham was already twiddling the keys to his Mercedes and looking impatient.

Barbara kissed Harry on the cheek. "Let me know how your gran gets on," she said.

Harry could have suggested her mother stay a night or two to see for herself how Gran was getting on. But the wedding must have made Harry sentimental, because she hugged them both instead, not sure when she'd see them again.

From her seat at a hay bale table, Harry ate her dessert and watched the wedding unfold. The couple circulated, hand-in-hand, laughing with their guests, many of whom were familiar to Harry. Several people came over and reminisced with Harry about the brief time they'd known her. Everything about the whole event felt real and comfortable.

When Jamie had first told her about Michael and Sarah's experiment in self-sufficiency, Harry couldn't imagine living such an uncertain lifestyle, depending on the land for your livelihood. Harry had a retirement account she'd been paying into since her very first job. She paid off her credit cards every month, saved for major purchases, and maintained an emergency savings account, which she was using now to see her through her current situation. Harry would be a nervous wreck if she lived like Michael and Sarah. And yet, seeing them together, Harry wondered if their lack of financial stability gave them a level of freedom. If all they had was each other, then that partnership had better be solid. And with those two, it looked like it was.

Gran had always told Harry "money can't buy love" and

Barbara had provided living proof. She'd married for financial security twice now, but Harry still wasn't sure if it was enough to satisfy her mother and bring her happiness. Harry enjoyed the perks of her own financial freedom, and she'd relished the treats that came along with Tom. But that hadn't been love, not even close. It had been nothing at all, really, just a flimsy excuse of a relationship, built on an invisible foundation, and it had come tumbling down in the first whiff of a breeze. Harry wondered idly if her mother was happy with the life she'd chosen, or if she'd even chosen it at all.

The lunch was winding down now. From a small marquee by the house, servers in jeans and white oxford shirts hurried with piles of dirty dishes. She'd looked for Jamie all through lunch. She wanted to tell him how amazing the food was, and how many compliments she'd heard from other guests. She saw him only once, just for a brief moment. He had been looking out at the guests, talking to a woman she vaguely recognized. She had caught his eye and smiled. He hadn't smiled back.

As the guests made their way over to the party, Harry thought she should probably excuse herself and go home. Sarah had been kind to invite her, and Harry had fulfilled Gran's wishes for photos. She looked for Sarah and Michael, deciding she too would thank them and head home for the night. She wished she could find Jamie just to say goodbye.

"Harry?" a voice said beside her.

She turned to see the woman who'd been talking to Jamie outside the marquee. She was about Harry's age, with a bright open face and wide open arms, which she used to pull Harry into a soft hug.

"You don't remember me, do you?"

Harry peered at the woman's face as she mentally peeled away the years since she'd lived in Hope. "Nicki?" she asked, the memories falling into place now.

"Michael's sister. The good-looking one." She threw her head back and howled with laughter so infectious it made Harry smile.

"I heard you were back."

"Just until Gran's better."

"She's a dynamo, your gran," Nicki said. "She never stops. I think she knows everyone within a twenty-mile radius of here."

"She won't let a little thing like a hip replacement slow her down, either."

"She misses you, though. She's always talking about you."

Harry smiled at the thought of Gran talking her up. "I'm glad I could be here for her. I've missed her, too."

"You ever think about moving back here?"

"To Hope?"

"It's not San Francisco, I know. But also... it's not San Francisco." Nicki grinned.

"I miss the trees and the countryside," Harry said. "And everyone's so friendly here, but San Francisco's my home now." Harry didn't add that it probably wouldn't be for long.

"You're brave to move away like that. I don't think I'd ever have the courage. Plus, how would my crazy family get along without me?" She laughed again. "No, I know it must seem like a small place where nothing ever happens, and maybe it is, but I can't imagine living anywhere else."

Harry looked around at the guests milling about the field. So many faces were familiar. There were lots of people she recognized, but even those she didn't know felt familiar to her. She'd been to weddings in the city where she'd known maybe one or two guests and clung to them all night as if they were flotsam from a shipwreck. But here she felt as if she were among friends.

"Your Gran's not the only one who's glad to see you, you know." Nicki gave Harry a sly smile and looked over Harry's shoulder.

Harry turned, trying to understand what she was saying, and there was Jamie. His shirt sleeves were rolled up to reveal the vine of colored ink that wrapped around his muscular forearm. He looked relaxed as he strode across the field, his long legs quickly closing the gap between them.

"You two were such a pair of lovebirds. I don't think I ever saw you apart."

Harry laughed. "Young love, eh?"

"It's a shame you didn't meet when you were older. It was so clear you were both destined for bigger things, but you were good together, weren't you?"

Harry nodded. "Life doesn't always give you exactly what you want when you want it."

"That's a fact. But I think sometimes it gives you a second chance."

Harry's eyes shot to Nicki, then back to Jamie. Is that what this was? A second chance? Maybe Nicki was right. Maybe Jamie had been the right person, just in the wrong time and place. But he was in the past. Wasn't he? Because even if the time was right now, the place was all wrong. Even if the next chapter of her life wasn't in San Francisco, it certainly wasn't here in Hope.

"Dance?" Jamie said, holding out his hand.

Harry glanced at Nicki, who raised her eyebrow. "I'd take him up on the offer if I were you. You might not get a second chance." She winked at Harry, raised her empty champagne glass, and headed for the bar.

Harry took Jamie's hand. Her fingers prickled when she touched his, clicking on a memory she'd long since stored away: his touch. The feeling of taking the hand of someone special.

"What was Nicki talking your ear off about?" Jamie asked as he led her to the floor.

Harry smiled to herself. "Just life," she said, and started to dance.

The band played every song from Harry's youth. She and Jamie danced and sang words she didn't know she remembered. Harry pulled out dance moves she hadn't used for decades, and Jamie mirrored her like they'd been dancing that way forever. By the time the band slowed things down, Harry's feet were on fire and her dress stuck to the moisture in the middle of her back. Jamie's hair stuck up in damp spikes. At some point, he'd undone another button on his shirt.

"To all the lovers out there," the singer said, her voice breathy. "We're available for weddings."

The crowd laughed and as the band played the opening notes of a familiar ballad, couples paired up, others left the floor, and people who'd been sitting on the sidelines suddenly found themselves pulled to their feet and led onto the dance floor. Harry made a show of looking tired. She ought to sit this one out. It was one thing to boogie the night away with Jamie, to laugh at one another's moves, to have fun. But slow dances always meant something, and Harry didn't want to send the wrong message. "Drink?" she asked.

Jamie took her hand and Harry was relieved he felt the same way and was leading her from the floor. But he didn't.

He held out his hands and took Harry's. He smiled. That smile. And when he invited Harry into his arms, she went.

Jamie's hands wrapped around her waist, and Harry's body moved in time with his, and when she rested her head on his shoulder, her senses relaxed with the familiar scent of somewhere she belonged.

It felt like being home.

CHAPTER TWELVE

IT WAS WELL after midnight when Harry flopped into the overstuffed armchair by Jamie's fireplace and stretched out her toes. "My poor feet," she said, folding an aching foot towards herself and rubbing it.

"Fancy a cuppa?" Jamie said.

Harry made a yummy groaning noise that Jamie seemed to interpret (correctly) as, "I would sell my own gran for a cup of tea right now."

As Jamie clattered around the kitchen, Harry stretched out in the chair, pushing her feet into the smooth pile of the old Persian rug. The room had a lived-in feel that seemed to wrap itself around her. The chair was soft and comfortable, but beneath the cushion molding around her bottom was the pressure of sturdy springs and a solid wooden base, something built to last. The rug looked like an antique and would have cost a small fortune in the ritzy Pacific Heights boutiques of San Francisco. But here it looked homey, like it belonged. A tall ficus filled a corner beside built-in bookcases stacked with cookbooks. From a top shelf, a spider plant lowered long thin arms down past two or three shelves, as if feeling for a safe, fertile spot to deposit its babies. The entire room had a welcoming, established feel to it. Even the marmalade-colored cat in the chair opposite looked like he'd spent his entire nine lives in that exact spot.

"How come you never got married?" Harry called into the kitchen.

The clattering of mugs stopped. A moment later, Jamie laughed. "Always the caterer, never the groom, I suppose."

"I'm serious. How come some lucky woman never snapped you up?"

Jamie wandered in and set two steaming mugs of tea on a small table beside her and pulled up a worn footstool. He perched on it and pulled her tired feet into his lap.

"I got my heart broken." He smiled at Harry half-heartedly.

Harry was taken aback. "I'm sorry, I..."

"Twice," he explained.

"Oh."

He took a breath. "Her name was Alexis. She was a fire-cracker. Still *is* a firecracker, actually. We were a hot couple, everyone said so. So we got married. Big to-do, hundreds of guests, celebrity chefs did the catering. We lasted six months."

"What happened?"

"We had fireworks, and they burned out. We got an annulment and went our separate ways."

"A split is a split," Harry said, repeating what Jamie had once told her.

He smiled. "In the case of that particular heartbreak, yes."

She didn't ask about the other heartbreak, the one she'd inflicted, and he didn't offer. A split was a split, after all. And yet here she was in Jamie Forrest's house, her feet in his hands. How had she not known he'd been married before? It was clear he didn't like talking about it, and she wondered if Gran knew, or if it was something Jamie always kept to himself. She hadn't exactly been open about Tom, had she? It wasn't the sort of information you just volunteered. Jamie hadn't asked, and she hadn't told. The same was true for him and Alexis, she supposed. One thing was clear, though, Jamie had a tender heart, and she needed to handle it with care.

"I think it's fair to say the wedding was a hit, don't you?" Harry said, changing the subject.

Jamie beamed. "Couldn't imagine a better celebration for those two."

"You must be exhausted," Harry said, as Jamie pressed his knuckles gently into the underside of her foot and found the exact spot that was crying out for attention.

"You've been on your feet all day, too."

"This desk-bound girl isn't used to it, but it was fun. Sarah was absolutely gracious. She was so kind to me. She had a few nice things to say about you, too."

Jamie gave her a wry grin. "Naturally."

"She raved about the lunch. Everyone did."

"Good."

"Your restaurant is going to be a hit. I'll look forward to trying it next time I'm here."

Jamie wrapped his hand around her feet but said nothing. Harry closed her eyes, feeling his firm fingers find all the right spots on her aching feet. It felt good to be touched again. She realized now how much she'd missed human contact since Tom's departure. Sometimes her life could be lonely. She'd never really minded coming home to an empty apartment, eating dinner for one, traveling BART without making eye contact, going for days without physical contact with another human. The nights with Tom had filled her need for touch; they'd just turned out to be empty. But coming home to this every night, coming home to someone like Jamie, would erase all those feelings of loneliness.

She sighed now, as Jamie's hands worked her feet. He hadn't had such a deft hand when they were together before, but there had never been the clumsy fumbling her friends had experienced with their first forays into love. She savored the familiarity of his touch, shaded with this new finesse.

She wondered idly what it would feel like to touch Jamie Forrest again. Would their bodies remember how to be together, a sort of muscle memory? She ran a finger around the rim of her mug and watched him move. They had been just a couple of kids back then, honing their skills on one another's inexperienced bodies. It had been puppy love, hadn't it? But love left footprints on a person's heart, and even though they were different people now, Harry wondered if Jamie's shoes would still fit the prints he'd left on her heart.

Jamie wasn't a skinny teenager anymore. He'd filled out into a fully-fledged man. But if he turned around and kissed her now, she bet it would be familiar. She sipped her tea, feeling the heat roll around her mouth, slipping down her throat and warming her insides. The way Jamie's kiss had once done.

Jamie's hands squeezed her ankle and moved up to massage her calves. She set down her tea, afraid she'd lose control and spill it. His touch was heavenly, and when he moved his hands up to her tired thighs, his face moving closer and closer to hers, she lifted herself from the chair to meet him.

And then she pulled away. A split is a split, Jamie had

said, and yet he'd hinted that he didn't feel the same way about their split. Had she misread him? It didn't matter. She was leaving soon, going back to California. She'd promised herself she wouldn't break Jamie's heart again, and the last thing she needed was a fling with another man she couldn't have. Everything about being here felt right, but everything about it was wrong. "I should go," she said.

"But I just made tea."

"This isn't tea, though, is it?"

He laughed. "Um, no. Definitely not tea."

"So, I should go."

He sat back on his heels, looking at her. And then he nodded.

He gave her his hand and pulled her up from the chair, led her to the door. "If we agree this means nothing, and no one is going to get hurt, can I at least kiss you goodnight?"

Harry nodded.

He leaned in slowly and pressed his lips against hers. His lips were just as she remembered them, soft and moist, pushing gently against hers, sealing her mouth with his, his tongue flicking gently on the doorstep of her mouth. Her hand felt the gap between his jeans and his shirt and, as her fingers grazed his skin, a little spark of electricity raced through his body and into hers. She pulled him towards her. His mouth was hungry against hers, as if it had waited a decade for this kiss. Everything about him was familiar, but changed. He was no longer a boy, he was all man now, and when she shifted her leg to let him closer still, she felt all the man push against her.

He slid his mouth from hers, leaving her gasping for his return. His lips caressed her jaw, and he buried his face into her neck, his ragged breath moving strands of her hair so that they tickled across her skin. A shock of prickly heat tore up her arm, down through her body, and exploded in between her thighs.

"I think I should go," she squeaked.

He whispered something she couldn't quite hear, something that sounded like, "Please stay."

"Goodnight," she breathed. "Thanks for the tea." And she hurried out into the cool night, every part of her burning hot.

CHAPTER THIRTEEN

ALL DAY SUNDAY, Jamie thought about Harry. He thought about Harry and that kiss. He thought about what would have happened if he hadn't let her go. When he'd pressed against her, Jamie hadn't been able to tell where he ended and Harry began. He had leaned into her, the scent of her hair reaching his nose, and let himself disappear. Everything about Harry fit. If he could have, he would have stayed that way all night. But then she'd left.

He tortured himself with a daydream about waking up on Sunday morning with Harry Belmont in his bed again, wondering how it would feel. He kept coming to the same conclusion. It would feel really, really good. He was an idiot to let her go.

But every time he let himself imagine the future, he pictured Harry getting in a taxi and going away, leaving him here to his old life, and going back to hers. And he knew. Letting her leave his house on Saturday night was the right thing to do for both of them.

So why did he regret it?

He reached for his phone. He should call her, talk about

what happened between them, what they ought to do now. But his hand stopped halfway. She needed space, breathing room to make the first move. He went to the kitchen, always the best place to think. But after the wedding, he had no energy to cook. Maybe he'd work on some ideas for the restaurant. Anything to take his mind off that kiss.

Determined to focus on anything but Harry, he cleared the kitchen table and gathered together a decade's worth of inspiration. He had notebooks and ring binders filled with recipes and menus, annotations scribbled in margins, sticky notes clinging to corners. Some recipes dated back to his time at culinary school, tested and refined over time. Others were his variations of new trends: potato rostis with pancetta and gruyere, a million variations on avocado toast, vegan Mushroom Wellington. He tapped his pen on a blank page of a notebook, then wrote "Local Goodness" at the top. He reached for his phone again. He should ask Harry about her favorite kits, get her input on his ideas. He thought about her face lighting up as she'd showed her the restaurant. He wanted to share every part of this new adventure with Harry.

Space, he reminded himself. *Got to give her space.* He stared at his notebook, his heart twisting just a little in his chest. Must focus. He jotted a list of his bestselling meal kits, making notes beside each of tweaks he might make in the restaurant. Should he keep a simple standard menu, supplemented with daily specials, or should he print a unique daily menu every day? He'd ask Harry.

Before he could reach for his phone again, he caught himself. This was ridiculous, this was *his* restaurant, *his* creation, he needed to do it his way. He pushed the phone to the far corner of the table and focused on his notes. He'd do a standing menu, he decided, nice and simple, six or seven of his most requested dishes available every day. He'd use the daily specials to test new creations, but his most loyal customers would always be able to get their favorites, just like they could with Local Goodness. And just like Local Goodness, all his ingredients would be sourced from the area.

He perked up in his seat. Local. That was the key. What if his meal kits and restaurant could work hand-in-hand? Local trout. Beef, chicken, lamb, all from local farms. Cheese, honey, herbs, vegetables were all easy to get from small producers in the area. He could get much of what he needed from Michael and Sarah. But how to define local? The sea was about sixty miles away, not exactly close. But if he sourced his fish from independent fishers, would that satisfy his customers? He made a note to do some informal market research.

He jumped when the phone rang, hoping it was Harry. But it wasn't Harry; it was Cameron McKenzie, following up on Jamie's decision about the property.

"Sorry to call on a Sunday, Jamie, but thought we should make a move early in the week."

Jamie tapped his pen on the notebook, running his eyes again down the list of menu items. This was it. This was the moment he must make a life-changing decision, trust his instincts, and take a risk. He wished Harry was here. "I want to make an offer," he said.

Cameron was thrilled. "Fantastic. I'll run some numbers and see how it looks."

"Do you have any idea what the other offers look like?" Jamie asked.

Cameron made a noise that sounded like the start of a laugh, but caught himself. "Um, as far as I know, yours is the first, but I'll make some enquiries to make sure we're competitive."

Jamie felt a familiar pang of apprehension. He'd felt the same thing before the opening of Slate, a sort of excitement and determination, undercut by a nagging sense of doom. He'd brushed it off that time, sure it was just new venture jitters, but he should have paid attention. The whole thing had been a catastrophe. It had wrecked his career, his marriage, and put a sizable dent in his confidence.

This time would be different, though. Last time he'd been too ambitious, an audacious concept in a high-rent spot with a temperamental business partner. This time he would rely on tested dishes in his familiar hometown, and only himself to depend on.

He wished he could talk this through with Harry. Ever since the moment he'd stood with Harry in the old village shop, he'd understood that her vision of the restaurant matched his. She got him, she understood him, and she had so many good ideas to help his vision become a reality. If he didn't tell her all this, if he didn't risk his tender heart by telling her how he felt, she'd be on a plane and six thousand miles away, and he would have to go it alone. But if he did tell her and she went away again anyway, he wasn't sure his heart would stand being broken in the same place twice.

No, his best plan was to stay focused on the new venture, show her he was serious about it and about her, and let her see for herself that this was where she belonged.

"Let's do it," he told Cameron.

Now he just needed to take the next step. As much as he'd love to be a one-man show, if he was going to make this business a success, he was going to need to hire help.

When Jamie's phone rang again, he was sure it would be Harry this time.

"You sound disappointed to hear from me," Michael said when Jamie answered.

"Aren't you supposed to be honeymooning or something?" Jamie asked.

"Sarah's at the hospital."

"What? Is she okay?"

"No, no. She took some wedding cake for Mrs. Belmont, that's all. I stayed to feed the chickens. And one of the goats is under the weather."

"And they say romance is dead."

"You know me. We'll get some romance in October and some proper time off, but for now it's business as usual."

"If you have a second, I could use some advice."

"Pub?"

"Can you spare the time?"

"I always have time for the hero of the day. All anyone's talked about since yesterday is your food."

"Good, because that's what I want to talk to you about."

At their usual table in The Butcher's Arms, Jamie laid out his notebook and the folder of applications. He told Michael about the interviews he'd done. "You've hired plenty of people in your time. Where do I start?"

Michael sat back and, for a moment, Jamie glimpsed the friend he used to know. When Michael had worked in The City, he made infrequent trips to Hope to see his family. He'd arrive just in time for last call on a Friday night, still tapping away on his phone, his shoulders scrunched up to his ears and his jaw set in a determined clench. He'd soften a little by Sunday, but in all those years, Jamie had never seen him truly relax. Not until he threw in his career and came back to set up his farm did Jamie see him look happy. And not until Sarah rode into Hope and snagged his heart did his friend really become his old self again.

"Start with your needs," Michael said. "What positions are you looking to fill and what skills and attributes do you need?"

"Well, I need someone I can trust to run Local Goodness. Ollie can process orders and deal with that side, so I'll need someone to handle deliveries and a manager to oversee the whole thing. They should be organized, but mostly I'm looking for someone who's good with people."

Jamie thought about some of his long-time customers, people like Jess and Callum. Over the years, he'd seen babies grow into schoolchildren, followed people through health issues, and had more than one cup of tea with a customer going through a bad time who just needed to talk. "They need to be part responsible businessperson, part delivery driver, and part therapist," Jamie said.

Michael nodded. "Well, you can get the business skills from their resumes and you can train them for the specifics, but the people side is more a feely thing. You'll have to gauge that from interviews."

"I did interview one person." He told Michael about Terry, the burly physicist who took care of his mother. "He checks all the boxes, but..."

"Sounds like he's your man," Michael said.

Jamie blew out his cheeks in a controlled sigh. Could he trust Terry to do the job he needed him to do? "It's going to be hard to give up that side of things. My customers have grown to trust me. Now they'll have a stranger knocking at their doors."

"But you can't manage Local Goodness, do the deliveries, *and* run a restaurant."

"If the restaurant was only open in the evenings, I could do the deliveries in the mornings."

"What about the day's kitchen prep? What about the

business side of the restaurant? What if someone calls in sick and you need to cover? You'll be overseeing two businesses. You're going to be spread thin enough as it is. And you said the main reason for this madness is to get back to cooking and creating. You can't do that if you're driving meal kits over hill and down dale."

Jamie pouted. "I thought you were my friend."

"Best you've ever had."

"Okay," Jamie said. "Terry it is."

"What about Ollie? Could he handle more responsibility?"

"I think so."

Michael smiled. "There you go, then. Who else do you need to hire?"

"Restaurant staff. It's a small place. I can probably get by with one kitchen helper and one server, at least to start."

Michael raised an eyebrow. "Really?"

"Why not?"

"I'm no pro, but it seems someone needs to greet guests, answer the phones, take orders, recommend wine, serve food, clear the tables, process bills. Are you sure one person can handle all that and give your customers their full attention, even in a small place?"

"Harry could manage some of it."

"Harry?"

Jamie felt his face pale. What was he talking about? Harry had been on his mind all day, but she wasn't part of his business plans. And yet, if he closed his eyes and pictured his restaurant dream, there she was, welcoming customers, circulating the tables, sneaking kisses behind the fridge.

"So, where exactly does Harry Belmont fit into this picture?"

Jamie shook his head. "Slip of the tongue. I've been talking to her about my plans, that's all. She has loads of good ideas. She's really lit a fire under me to go after what I want."

"She always could do that. And what is it that you do want?"

"To cook again. It's always been about the cooking. You know that."

Michael nodded. "Two questions then."

"Fire away."

"Is this restaurant your dream or Harry's?"

"Mine."

"Sure? Because you know chasing someone else's dream doesn't work."

Jamie hesitated. Slate, with its big concept and showy menu, had not been his dream, and Michael knew it. But this was different. Home was the restaurant he'd always wanted. It just happened that Harry shared his vision. "That's two questions already. And yes, I'm sure."

"Can I have a third question then?"

Jamie shrugged.

"Is your dream the restaurant?"

"You just asked me that."

"I didn't finish. Is your dream the restaurant or is it Harry Belmont?"

Jamie twisted his mouth, as if considering the question, but he already knew the answer. "Is there any reason I can't have both?"

"Mixing business with pleasure?"

"This is different," Jamie said.

"Then I think that's a question for Harry."

~

FROM THE WINDOW of her old childhood bedroom, Harry watched Jamie walk through the village to The Butcher's Arms. All day she'd waited for him to call so they could talk about the moment that had zipped between them. All day, she'd wondered what might have happened if she hadn't left. And in between those thoughts, an idea kept bobbing to the surface. What if I stayed? What if I came and lived with Gran? What if I took that second chance?

But Jamie never called. And now she watched him walk to the pub. He never so much as glanced at Gran's cottage. He never even gave her a second thought.

CHAPTER FOURTEEN

HARRY WAS UP EARLY on Monday morning. She had an interview with the company in Boston after lunch, and even though she was prepared, she was nervous. The hospital had called to say Gran would be released later, and Harry knew she was inching toward the end of her visit. After the incident with Jamie, it was probably best she went, anyway. And that meant finding a job to go home to. She hoped the interview went well.

After breakfast, Harry dressed in her oldest clothes and slipped out into the small square of back garden behind Gran's cottage. A bit of weeding would take her mind off the interview. Gran had bemoaned the weeds that had taken advantage of her inability to bend. She swore she'd be back in her garden to tackle them as soon as she could, and Harry had promised to make a start. Instead, she'd been spending her spare time with Jamie. Had that really been the best use of her time?

Harry took hold of a grassy-looking thing and pulled. The weed resisted for a moment, clinging to its home, before the roots loosened and it came away in Harry's hand. She moved to the next and did the same.

She should probably tell Jamie about Gran coming home. He'd offered to drive her, but that had been before Saturday night. Now she wasn't sure if he even wanted to see her. Something had happened with Jamie, first something good, then something not so good, and she needed to figure out what exactly it was.

That day he'd shown her the restaurant, she'd sensed a spark between them. And for those few moments that she'd stood with him in the derelict room, so filled with beautiful possibilities, she had a glimpse of a different life. Home, work, love, all within the confines of this silly old village.

She reached for another weed, a tall thing with spiked leaves and the beginnings of a yellow flower head. She pulled at it absently, waiting to feel the roots give, but the thing didn't budge.

And then she'd gone home with Jamie after the wedding, and she'd been so close to spending the night and rekindling that old flame. And if she'd stayed, her whole life would have been turned upside down. Free, independent, self-sufficient Harry Belmont would be just like her mother.

No matter what Gran said about Harry not being like Barbara, coming home still felt like defeat. Harry had left Hope at eighteen and sworn she wouldn't come back. Now, she had lost her job, been dumped by a cheating boyfriend, and faced starting all over again when she returned. Moving back to Hope, when she had little to lose, would be a compromise, like throwing in the towel and taking the easy route.

But Jamie offered a tantalizing lure, something real and steady, a solid foundation on which to build a new life. Was the pull she felt toward him a true attraction, or was she just allowing herself to fall into a safety net, just like her mother always did?

She tugged again on the stubborn weed, but it refused to give. She stuck her trowel into the damp earth and tried to loosen the roots. But the little weed had decided it was happy where it was, and it wouldn't leave without a fight. Harry dug deeper.

The trouble was, Jamie or no Jamie, Harry could picture herself here. Every spot in the village held a memory. The old miller's cottage was where her school friend had lived. At the stop in front of the post office, she'd caught the local bus a thousand times to get away from the village. The village shop—soon to be Jamie's new restaurant—was where Gran always sent her when she ran out of bread or tea, or needed a safety pin or sticky tape. The old stone fountain was where she'd kissed Jamie for the last time before she'd left for university. It was all in her past now, but somehow she felt alive here.

Her life in San Francisco felt like someone else's flimsy existence. And Tom had not been real. Everything about him had been a lie, a stupid lie. What an idiot she had been. And she'd lost her job because of him. What kind of twenty-first century woman threw away her career for a man? Especially a man who didn't love her. That was definitely something her mother would do.

And yet, she could imagine a life with Jamie; she could visualize the restaurant; she could see herself popping over to check on Gran, helping her on her quest to defeat the weeds. And when she pictured a life back in Hope, it felt right. When she pushed aside the feelings of failure, the defeat of returning to the place she swore she'd never live again, it felt like slipping into a favorite sweater, the kind that fit in all the right places, that flattered her shape, that hung at just the right length, enclosed her body in its cozy fibers, the kind that didn't itch.

She had Gran to think about, too. Seeing her in the hospital, weak and in pain, her inner feistiness taking a hit, had brought it home to Harry that her grandmother was getting old. Harry tried to push the thought aside as too morbid to consider, but the reality hit hard. Her time with Gran was growing short and the opportunities to visit were numbered. One day, she would say goodbye to Gran, and it would be for the last time. One day, Gran would need her, and she wouldn't be able to get there in time.

She dug her hands deeper in the earth, tugging at the roots of the weed. She felt a snap and loosened the earth a little more. And when she tugged at the weed again, it came away in her hand, roots dangling, leaving a hole in the ground where it had once been so firmly planted. Satisfied with a job well done, Harry went inside to prepare for her interview, and to tell Jamie that Gran was coming home.

THE INTERVIEW with the firm in Boston went better than Harry could have hoped. Her interviewers asked tricky questions and Harry answered them all. When Jamie picked her up to get Gran, Harry felt as if she finally had a grip on the day. As they drove into town, she told Jamie about the interview.

"So, you're not going back to San Francisco?"

"Just to tie up loose ends, with luck."

He was quiet for a long while, focusing on the road ahead. Then he asked, "Ever think about moving back here?"

Harry didn't answer. Her mind whirred as it read between the lines and tried to decipher what he was really asking. Was he asking her with interest or making conversation? "I've thought about it," she ventured.

He jerked his head to face her, then just as quickly turned back to the road. That looked like interest to Harry.

"About Saturday," they both said at the same time, then laughed nervously.

"You go," said Harry.

"No, you," said Jamie.

"I had a really nice time," she said.

"Me too."

"I'm sorry I left."

"Me too."

"But..." She didn't know what to say next. But I don't want to hurt you? But, I'm leaving in a week, so where could this go? "But, you didn't call."

"Neither did you."

"But, I wanted to."

"So did I."

"But..." Here she was again, stuck in the same old spot. "But, I'm leaving in a week. Where could this go? You live here, I live there."

"But you could live here."

"I could," Harry said. "But I don't."

"But you could," Jamie said as he pulled the car to the curb outside the hospital entrance.

I could, Harry thought. But I don't.

In her pocket, Harry's phone rang, jolting her from her thoughts. She thought she was seeing things when "Tom" flashed on her screen. She stared at his name, the spike of the T, the casual flow of the O and M. It was a sharp name, a spiky name, a name that belonged to someone who didn't dance and laugh with her all night, who didn't leave her feeling the same satiated glow as a day at the beach, who had never taken her home and made her a cup of tea, massaged her feet, whose kitchen she had never entered to cook a meal together.

She clicked the phone off. Whatever Tom had to say, it could wait. She didn't want to hear his voice today, especially not right now. He had not earned the right to be a priority. Because she had never been his.

She stuck the phone in her pocket. "Sorry," she told Jamie. "Maybe we can talk later. I want to…" Her phone rang again. "I need to take this," she said, and hopped from the car, half furious at Tom and half-relieved to excuse herself from the tricky conversation with Jamie.

"What is it?" she snapped into the phone as she stomped toward the hospital entrance. Only when she heard a long pause on the other end of the line did she realize it might not be Tom calling again.

"Harry?" said a woman's voice. "This is Judith."

The voice was jarring, the drawling accent so foreign after the clipped English voices that had surrounded her these past weeks. It took Harry a moment to process the voice and put a face and a place to Judith, the HR director from her old job.

"Harry, there've been some developments since you left here. I wonder if we could talk."

Developments? That sounded ominous. "Sure," said Harry, her own California-isms coming back. "I'm all ears."

"Actually, would you be able to come in and meet with me, with a small group actually?"

Harry stepped aside to let a man on crutches inch his way to a waiting taxi. "A small group? What's this about?"

"I'd rather speak in person."

Harry felt a prickle of annoyance. Judith had been pretty snide about dropping bad news to Harry, making her feel like an idiot about Tom, and sliding in a not very subtle dig about Meredith. "That's not possible at the moment. I'm in England, taking care of my grandmother."

"Oh. Is she okay?"

"She's much better. Thanks."

"When will you be back?"

Harry hesitated. She had a ticket booked. In just ten days, assuming Gran was able to manage by herself, she'd be on her way home, back to her life, free to go into the office to meet with Judith. But suddenly she didn't want to put those plans into words. It would make them feel final. "I don't know," Harry said.

Judith was quiet for a moment. "Can you hold for a minute?" Before Harry could answer, soft jazzy music eased from the phone. She barely had time to be annoyed about Judith's brusque attitude when she was back. The background hum had gone, and Harry was sure Judith had put her on hold so she could close her office door. This was serious. Harry hurried into the hospital lobby and headed for a quiet corner, intrigued.

"Here's the thing," Judith said. "There's been a complaint filed. Against Tom."

"What kind of complaint?"

Judith hesitated. "Sexual harassment."

Harry laughed. She couldn't help herself. "Tom?" Tom had many faults, but sexual harassment? That didn't sound like him.

Judith wasn't laughing. "An employ-ee filed a grievance. She and Tom had been in some kind of relationship and she learned certain things."

Harry blinked. What was Judith saying?

"And then, of course, you were mentioned. So I was hoping to talk to you. If this is true, if Tom has been abusing his position to garner sexual favors, these are very serious allegations."

"Sexual favors? He wasn't 'garnering sexual favors.'"

But even as she spoke the words, Harry had a sinking feeling. What an idiot she'd been. Because, of course, if Tom was cheating on his wife with her, what would stop him cheating on Harry with someone else? Harry could see it now. She had fallen for a serial philanderer. Not serial, she thought. That suggested one philandering after another. Tom had been way more ambitious than that. Tom had been more of a *synchronous* philanderer.

But a sexual predator? Tom? She thought about his hires. He got a lot of credit for hiring women, showing those nerdy tech guys that women were more than capable of taking their precious jobs. Harry had loved that about him. But now she saw a pattern. Yes, he selected his team based on professional skills, but he looked for other talents in his female employees, too.

So that's why he'd called her, trying to get ahead of Judith and the sexual harassment claim, trying to lure Harry over to his camp. What a weasel. "I'll be back at the end of next week," Harry said. "I'll come in and talk then."

Gran was waiting in a wheelchair when Harry got up to the nurse's station. She looked tired, but her eyes lit up when she saw Harry. "For God's sake, get me out of here and get me a decent cup of tea," she said.

Harry wheeled Gran out of the hospital to where Jamie waited. He hopped out when he saw them, and together they helped Gran out of the wheelchair and into the front seat. As they reached to steady her, their hands touched and their eyes met. Jamie winked, and Harry's insides curled into what felt like a smile. Because this was life, wasn't it? Working with a partner to help an elderly relative, spending lazy evenings cooking together, sharing ideas about a new venture. Love wasn't just about the physical. It was about the teamwork. Love wasn't spiky and truncated. It was comfortable and safe, like a favorite armchair, like home.

"SO," Gran said with an impish smile, when she and Harry were finally alone, "what have you been up to while I've been away?"

Harry's cheeks flushed, like she was a child caught doing something she shouldn't. She busied herself tucking the blanket around Gran's legs and making sure her tea and puzzle book were within easy reach.

"I went to a wedding," she said, pulling out her phone and scrolling through the pictures.

"Ooh, doesn't she look lovely," Gran said of a picture of Sarah. "Would you look at that dress?"

"I wish you could have been there, Gran."

"I'm enjoying it through you just as much."

"That's a fib, and you know it. You would have been on the dance floor all night."

Gran chuckled. Harry flipped through pictures of the bridesmaids, the hay bale chapel, the reception tables set out in the orchard, and the old friends she had reconnected with. At the end was a selfie she didn't remember taking with Jamie on the dance floor. She pulled the phone away. "That's all of them," she said.

"Looks like you had a nice time," Gran said. "You'll miss everyone when you go home."

Home. The word hit Harry in the core. She looked at Gran, expecting to see a warning, some disapproval of Harry's behavior. Because it was clear to Harry that wily old Gran knew exactly which old friend in particular she'd been catching up with and how.

"Well, I'm not going anywhere just yet," Harry said. "I've got to get you well first."

"Yes, well, what I need most of all is a good, long nap. The hospital is the worst place to get any rest. Now, what I always do when I have a lot on my mind is to take myself out for a nice long walk."

Harry glanced at Gran's leg, the walker by her chair, the bottles of pain medication on the table. Gran followed her gaze. "I've got a new hip now. I'll be out making big decisions again before you know it. Now get yourself out so I can get some rest."

Harry smiled and kissed Gran on the forehead. "Don't open the door to any strange men while I'm gone."

"I should be so lucky," Gran said, and closed her tired eyes.

CHAPTER FIFTEEN

HARRY DIDN'T PAY much attention to where she was walking. She just followed the path in front of her. So it didn't surprise her when she arrived at the bench looking out over the Hope Valley. She sat down, feeling the cool dampness of the wood beneath her. The air was chilly today, but it seemed to wrap around her like a light blanket, the humidity somehow making her feel warmer than she ought to be. Across the valley, puffy white clouds hung low in a robin's-egg blue sky. The sky here was different from the California sky. There the sky was a distant thing, not of the human world. But here it seemed closer, the elements more immediate, making Harry feel like part of something bigger than just herself.

What would it be like to live here again? Could she do it? She'd been away for more than a decade. The village had changed in that time—new people moving in, life moving progressively faster. But in many ways it was the same. Same buildings, same long-time residents, same views of the surrounding hills. As a teenager that sameness had felt like a prison to Harry and staying here would have meant stagnating, being trapped in the person she was then, with no room to change and grow.

She'd been right to move away. Her view of the world had expanded. She'd met people from all over the world, celebrated the diversity of human life, grown to accept and understand the differences in people. She had the space to bloom into the person she was truly meant to be. Could she now move back to a place that was small and familiar?

In San Francisco, as with all the big cities she'd called home, she'd felt like part of a big, colorful mosaic. But in reality, she'd been just another fragmented piece, separated from all the other pieces by the isolating cement of city life. She could be anyone she wanted to be in the city, but somewhere along the way, she had lost sight of Harry. Now she belonged nowhere.

She thought about the wedding, how she'd walked in a stranger and been swept up into the community. Nicki had sought her out and included her in the conversations. Sarah had made a point of finding her and asking after Gran. She'd even taken time the day after her own wedding to take a slice of cake to the hospital to make sure Gran was included in their celebration. People had talked to Harry, asked questions, been interested in who she was, instead of talking all about themselves and looking for ways the connection could help *them*. Networking was part of life in the city. It was how Harry had stayed employed, how she'd found her apartment, made friends, learned how to navigate each city. But it often felt like brief sparks of connection that came and went on the path to somewhere else. She felt like she *belonged* in the city only because, like everyone around her, she *didn't* belong. If she moved back to Hope, would the opposite be true? Would she feel like an outsider because she was different, or would the community wrap around her and pull her in to its folds? Would she feel stifled by that, or would it feel like coming home?

Home.

Gran was right. Harry wasn't like her mother. She hadn't come here because she was out of options. If she came home now, it would be by choice. Moving back wouldn't be a step backwards, but more like coming full circle, having been out in the world and becoming who she was meant to be. And maybe this Harry was meant to be here.

She could find work here, apply for the job in London and work remotely, even set up a consulting business working from home. She could stay with Gran at first, help her around the house. It would be lovely to spend more time with her. She'd be half an hour from town and all the amenities it offered, and she could take this walk and sit on this bench any day of the week.

And then there was Jamie.

"I thought I might find you here."

Harry startled at the sound of a voice. That's another thing that was different. She would never allow someone to sneak up on her in the city. On the streets, she was always vigilant and aware of her surroundings. She looked up and there stood Jamie, as if thinking about him had called him into existence.

"Mind if I join you?" Jamie asked.

Harry patted the bench beside her, unable to form words. She had just been thinking about Jamie, and then he'd appeared. Was it a sign?

"I had a feeling I might find you here," he said.

"We've been here a few times before, haven't we?"

He smiled. "We certainly have."

They both gazed out across the valley. Harry's mind flitted back to all the times she'd spent here with Jamie. She wondered if he was thinking about them, too.

"You look sort of pensive," Jamie said at last.

Harry laughed. "I've been thinking about some things, yes."

"Penny for them?"

She shook her head and smiled. "Not yet." Not until she was done thinking this through. If she came home, it needed to be a logical decision, not made fuzzy by emotion. A decision whose edges weren't blurred by the lovely, tender vibe that was radiating from Jamie and softening her thoughts.

"I've been doing some thinking myself," Jamie said. "And I need your opinion."

"Mine?" Harry asked. "Why me?"

Jamie beamed. "Because I trust you."

Harry felt a glow in her belly. After all the ways she'd found to doubt herself after what she was now calling "The Tom Incident," Jamie's faith warmed her.

"First some news. My offer was accepted. The property is mine."

Harry threw her arms around Jamie and hugged him. "That's fantastic."

"It is. And I've been thinking about what you said." He inched down the bench and Harry felt his warmth beside her. "About following my dreams and doing what's important to me."

"The restaurant."

"Right. But the thing is, I love Local Goodness. I love

sharing my recipes with my customers, I love knowing I'm helping them to love cooking."

"It would be tough to run both."

"Unless I combine them."

Harry frowned.

"I have this idea," Jamie said, "and I need someone to tell me if it's the worst idea I've ever had."

Harry laughed. "That winter you and Michael raced one another down Longline fields on biscuit tin lids and you couldn't stop and plowed into the stone wall. That was the worst idea you've ever had. I find it hard to imagine this one could be worse."

"You haven't heard it yet," he said, but his hand automatically brushed the wiggly half-moon scar at the hairline above his right temple. "So here's what I'm thinking. I have a small standard menu for Home, a dozen or so main dishes that customers know they can always get. I'll supplement that with three daily specials, based on whatever's in season and available from my producers."

"I don't know much about running a restaurant, but that sounds fairly standard."

"Right, but here's where it's not standard. What if I shared the recipes for some of those go-to favorites with my customers so they can recreate them at home?"

"Share the recipes?" Harry said, finally catching on to what Jamie was saying. "Won't that give away all your secrets?"

"Not just the recipes. Meal kits."

"So people could order their favorites and make them at home?"

"Exactly."

"But then why would they bother getting dressed up,

leaving their cozy houses to pay, what, two, three times more for the same thing?"

"That's what makes me worried it's a stupid idea."

Harry shrugged. "Sounds like you don't need my help at all."

Jamie held up a finger. "Except. If you do it yourself, you have to, well, do it yourself. You stand at the stove, follow a recipe, maybe you're tired and accidentally miss a step. Or you get distracted and burn the salmon *en croute*." He gave Harry his best cheeky grin. She swatted him in return. "Then you have to wash all those dishes. And even though it's a good meal, it's not quite as good as it is in the restaurant."

"Like when you go on holiday and have an amazing new food, so you take some home with you and it never tastes the same."

"Right. But why doesn't it taste the same if it's the exact same food?"

Harry thought about the time she and Tom had gone to Hawaii for a long weekend. They'd sat on the hotel's lanai eating freshly caught kampachi, grilled with a macadamia crust, and drinking real pineapple cocktails. The trade winds rippled through the palm trees, the moonlight glinted off the waves, and the balmy night air was rich with the scent of flowers. It truly had been paradise. Harry had brought home a fresh pineapple in a box and the following weekend she'd gone down to Japantown in San Francisco and found fresh kampachi. She'd recreated the dinner and she and Tom had eaten it overlooking the city.

But it hadn't been the same. The air was different, the ambience was all off, and the fog had rolled in, making the air cold and damp. Tom had been different, too. He'd been antsy, not relaxed, like he'd been in Hawaii. He'd kept looking at his phone all night until Harry had finally called him out. Instead of laughing at how stressed out he was, he'd told her he needed to go. She hadn't stopped him.

"When you go out to a restaurant, there's an ambience," she said to Jamie. "It's more relaxed, an event, not just cooking a meal. It's special."

"Exactly," said Jamie.

"So, people can come to Home, have a great meal and an experience."

"Then they can subscribe to Local Goodness to get the meal kits delivered."

"Makes their everyday cooking easier."

"And when they want to taste the meal done right, or make it special..."

"You'll have a table waiting for them."

Harry thought about the salmon *en croute* experience again. Even when she'd mastered it herself, it had never tasted as good as the night Jamie had come over and cooked it for her. There was the wine, the company, the relaxed mood of sitting around with her feet up, chatting and laughing with Jamie. She'd take that experience any time over eating at home alone. And goodness knows she'd done that enough times to know it was the pits.

"The restaurant can generate business for Local Goodness, and Local Goodness can advertise the restaurant," she said.

"Exactly."

"Maybe the specials could highlight a different local producer each week," she said. "Or the menu could include a list of sources of the ingredients, something to bring the local element of Local Goodness into the restaurant."

"Ooh, I like that idea."

"We'll need a social media campaign," Harry said. "We

could feature all the producers and connect with their established audiences. Post pictures of the homey details, really play up that 'home for dinner' feel. We can also work the exclusive angle, not in the high end 'you need to book six months in advance and re-finance your house to eat here' way, but maybe play up the home idea, give the feeling that eating there is like being invited to dinner at a friend's house. '*Mi casa es su casa*' or 'Home is where the heart is.' Something like that."

Jamie stared at her, and she realized she hadn't stopped talking for long enough to hear any of his ideas. "Sorry," she said. "Getting ahead of myself."

"No, it's fantastic. Do you think it could work?" Jamie looked like a little kid again. His eyes were bright, and his smile filled his whole face. Everything about him made Harry smile.

"I do."

Jamie slid across the bench and scooped Harry up into his arms, making her laugh. She thought briefly that she should put a stop to this before anything else started. But when he covered her mouth with his and kissed the laughter back down, Harry didn't pull away. Instead, she kissed his back and thought that maybe she could stay here just a little while longer.

Once he'd set her down again, they walked back into the village, Jamie talking a mile a minute about all his ideas. Harry listened in silence. If Jamie thought she wasn't taking in what he was saying, he was wrong. His words wrapped around her, seeped into her pores, slid deep into her core, and took up residence in her heart. Every word he spoke was infused with passion, and she could picture the restaurant clearly. He was really going to make a go of it. Not just open another same-old restaurant, but create something that was truly his, like she'd always known he could.

Harry felt a strange sense of pride, not in herself, but in Jamie. He was following his dreams, just as they'd always planned. She wanted to be there to see them unfold, but before she told him that, she had to be sure.

CHAPTER SIXTEEN

JAMIE SAT at his kitchen table and sorted a stack of job applications into piles. At Michael's suggestion, he'd posted his positions online, and now he had enough applications to paper every wall in the new restaurant. He had wait staff applicants with multiple degrees, and candidates for manager whose only experience was a Saturday job at The Gap. His stack of inappropriate applicants was at least double the height of the stack of possibilities, but he'd given Terry a chance and Jamie felt confident he would prove to be a good choice.

He wished he could ask Harry to help. He hadn't stopped thinking about their conversation on the bench, and how enthusiastic she'd been about his new idea. Mostly, though, he kept thinking about how she kept saying "we." *We* could do this, and *we* need to do that. He was dying to talk more, but he needed to give her time with her gran. Plus, Michael's probing questions still lingered among his thoughts. For as long as Jamie could remember, cooking for others had been his dream. Harry's image of the little bistro serving comforting food to regular guests fit his nature perfectly. It was his dream; it just happened that Harry shared it. But Harry had always been his dream, too. He couldn't deny that. So why couldn't he have both? Why shouldn't he tell her his true feelings? Why shouldn't he ask her to stay?

A flicker in his chest caught his attention. A little twang of warning seared through the scar where his heart had broken, not once, but twice. He'd heard somewhere that scar tissue was always thicker than the surrounding skin. The scar on his forehead told him that was true, but invisible scars didn't work the same way. Harry had made the first scar, but Alexis had ripped it open in exactly the same spot. He didn't think he could stand to have it opened again.

He needed advice. His mum would tell him to steer clear of Harry, and he didn't want to hear that. Harry's gran always had sage advice, but he couldn't ask her. As an only child, he had no one to turn to for sisterly advice. But he did have a big sister he could borrow. He reached for his phone.

"Nicki," he said, when Michael's sister answered. "Any chance you have a few minutes for a bit of sisterly advice?"

"For you, always, but I have guests arriving any minute. Can you come over around seven?"

"Perfect."

"Anything I need to know to prepare?"

"It's a matter of the heart. I'll leave it at that."

"Ah," Nicki said.

Just from that little one-syllable word, Jamie got the feeling Nicki already knew he was coming to talk about Harry.

"I'll see you at seven," he said.

"Feel free to bring treats."

Jamie finished sorting his applications, sent interview requests to his top three candidates for each job, then whipped up a batch of the sun-dried tomato and goat cheese tartlets Nicki had raved about at the wedding. By the time he arrived at the open back door to Sunnydale, the bed-and-breakfast Nicki ran, she was already at the kitchen table waiting for him.

Michael was with her. So was Sarah. And Nicki's assistant, Jennie. And as Jamie took a step inside, Ollie wandered in behind him.

"All right, Bossman?" Ollie said, already eyeing the plate Jamie had in his hand.

"What's all this?" Jamie asked. "An intervention?"

"Of sorts, yes," Nicki said.

"I was hoping for a friendly chat, bit of advice."

"And advice you shall get. Have a seat."

Jamie plunked onto a stool and looked around the circle of faces, all staring intently at him.

"It's about Harry," Nicki said.

"Oh." Jamie felt himself deflate. He'd been right, of course, that Nicki was one step ahead of him, but still, he'd hoped to have a quiet personal chat with her. This was not what he had in mind.

Nicki leaned in to him, resting a soothing hand gently on his knee. "Jamie, petal. Ever since she arrived, you've been mooning around this village like a dog that forgot where he buried his bone." Jamie started to protest, but Nicki held up her hand. "Sorry to air all your dirty laundry in front of everyone, but we're all family here."

Jamie frowned. "Okay, so what do you suggest I do about it?"

"I think," said Ollie, "that you should just tell her she completes you, that when you realize you want to spend the rest of your life with someone, you want the rest of your life to start as soon as possible. Tell her you'll always have Paris."

"Ollie," Jamie said. "Those are movie lines. You know they only work in movies, don't you? Plus, didn't Bogie say the Paris thing as he was letting her leave with her husband?"

"Not the point, Bossman. It's romantic. And you won't know if they work unless you try."

"Cook her a nice dinner," Jennie, Nicki's assistant, said. "Make it all romantic with twinkly lights and soft music. Women love that."

"Do they?" Ollie asked.

"They do, actually," Jennie said, and immediately blushed.

"Maybe the restaurant would be the perfect spot for it," Sarah said quietly. "You could clear a little space, clean it up, make it nice. That would be really romantic."

Jamie looked at Michael. "Are you going to help me here, mate?"

Michael opened his mouth, but Nicki leaned across him. "You have to go for it. If you don't, you're going to kick yourself for letting the one that got away get away again."

Jamie lifted an eyebrow. "Should I really be taking dating advice from you?"

"Yes," Nicki said. "I may not be out fishing every day, but when the right one comes along, I'll be ready with my hook. In the meantime, I'm more than happy to dole out advice."

Jamie softened. He shouldn't have goaded Nicki about dating. Everyone knew there'd only ever been one person for her, but it comforted him to know that didn't mean she would never love again.

"Let's face it," Nicki added. "If it hadn't been for me, my brother here would have let Sarah go."

"Is that true?" Sarah asked.

Michael fixed Nicki with a firm gaze, deftly dodging his new wife's question. He waved his hands to settle everyone down. "This is all great advice," he said, "but in the end it's down to our friend here. Let's not forget he's had his heart broken before."

"Thanks a lot, mate," Jamie said. If he'd been looking for gentle reassurance, he had definitely come to the wrong place.

"Does Harry know about Alexis?" Nicki asked.

"Yes," Jamie said. "For the most part."

Nicki frowned. "Which part?"

"That we were together, married... briefly."

"If you decide to go for it, we're behind you all the way," Michael said, clapping Jamie on the shoulder. "But Nicki's right about one thing. Anyone only has to look at you to see you're still in love with her. So, either way, you need to do something about it. Either take the chance and tell her how you feel, or let her go and move on."

Jamie stared at the group around him. They were either the best friends a person could ask for, or the worst. At the end of the day, maybe they were both. And maybe they were exactly the kind of friends he needed.

"Well?" Nicki said, raising one eyebrow like she wasn't going to let him leave without giving her an answer.

Jamie sighed and took out his phone. As he scrolled to Harry's number, he sensed everyone in the kitchen grow still until all he could hear was the novelty cat clock ticking on the kitchen wall. That, and his heart thudding in his chest like it might explode.

"Harry?" he said when she answered the phone. "It's

me." Nicki rolled her eyes. "I was wondering if you were free for dinner on Saturday night."

"Of course," Harry said. "I'd love that."

"How about seven at the restaurant?"

"Which one?"

"My restaurant. Home."

She laughed. "Okay."

Jamie beamed at the line of expectant faces. "Great, then it's a date."

He wasn't entirely sure if he'd hung up the call before the kitchen erupted in a cheer. He was going on a big date with Harry Belmont. His heart gave a little tremor. It had either skipped a beat with excitement or tripped and missed a beat with dread. Either way, he would find out for sure whether Harry Belmont would be part of his future... or just the saddest two chapters of his history.

CHAPTER SEVENTEEN

BY SATURDAY, Gran was moving around like her old self again. "Better than my old self, really," she told Harry. It was still hard for her to bend, but she had no problem standing to deadhead her roses and instructing Harry on which plants to trim and which weeds to pull. Harry enjoyed the "pottering," as Gran called it. It was lovely to be out in the warm sun, and the work kept her mind off her approaching departure. But it didn't keep her mind off Jamie.

She was both nervous and excited about their dinner date. Something was happening between them and she needed more time to see what it was and what, if anything, she wanted to do about it. She might have changed her ticket and stayed longer, except the company in Boston had called and offered her the job. She had a week to accept the offer and another two weeks to wrap up her life in San Francisco and move to the opposite coast. It wasn't enough time to make one big, life-changing decision, never mind two. But the closer she got to leaving, the less she felt ready to go.

"It's been lovely having you here," Gran said as she snipped a faded rose.

"It's been lovely being here," Harry said. She leaned into a rose hip, snipped, missed, and watched as a perfectly beautiful blossom tumbled to the ground.

Gran stifled a gasp. "And you have a new chapter to look forward to," she said, reaching for a dead stem.

"Hmm," Harry said. In the past, she'd looked forward to her new contracts and fresh starts, but this one felt different. Everything about the job in Boston was right for her, and yet she was hesitant about the new adventure. She didn't mind the packing, the moving, or the starting all over. But when she pictured herself alone in a city where she knew no one, a deep emptiness crept in. The only saving grace was that she'd be closer—by a few hours—to Gran. "I'll be close enough for long weekend visits," Harry said. "I'll be here so often you'll be sick of the sight of me."

"You'll be very welcome anytime," Gran said, and gave Harry a knowing smile.

"You're being coy, Gran. If you have something to say, let's hear it."

But Gran just threw up her hands. "I've never interfered in your life, Harry, and I'm not going to start now."

Harry wished Gran *would* interfere. She could use some advice right about now. As soon as Jamie had invited her to dinner, Harry was certain he was going to ask her to stay. Part of her wanted to say yes, and the other part was terrified. She ran again over the words she'd practiced in the mirror. They all sounded wrong, overdramatic, insincere. But as long as she could get her point across to Jamie, that was all that mattered. She ran through the presentation slides she'd created in her mind to help keep her thoughts straight:

Slide 1:

- Love spending time with Jamie
- Excited to support his new venture

Slide 2:

- Essential he put whole heart into restaurant
- Essential she not ditch great opportunity for silly daydream

Slide 3:

- Are they sure they have something between them?

Slide 4:

- Can a person ever be sure about anything?

She needed to know if he was sure, or at least mostly sure, because being together meant her giving up the opportunity in Boston, changing everything about her life, and she needed to be sure. Or mostly sure.

That was the problem with love: it didn't come with any guarantees. They called it "falling" in love because it entailed letting go of anything solid and certain, and taking a chance that it would all work out. Was she really ready to do that? Was she ready to risk giving it all up for a chance with Jamie?

She was. She was sure she was. At least she thought she was sure she was.

She snipped off another perfectly healthy rose and swore under her breath. She wasn't sure of anything.

When Harry came downstairs that evening to leave for her date with Jamie, Gran's face lit up. "Well, don't you look lovely."

Harry giggled. Every time she thought about the "date," a different sensation came over her. Sometimes she giggled like the teenager she'd been on her first date with Jamie. Sometimes her face flushed and her body tingled as if Jamie were standing right in front of her. And sometimes her knees buckled under the crushing uncertainty of what she was about to do.

"Your mother's popping over," Gran said. "She just rang."

"Popping over from where?" Her mother had to pick tonight, of all nights, to make an impromptu visit?

"They're stopping on their way up to Scotland. Guilt visit, I imagine. She should be here any minute."

"Would it be bad if I dashed out before she came?"

Gran grinned. "Yes. But I won't tell her where you are."

Harry kissed Gran on the cheek. "Gran, you are a peach."

The smile her grandmother gave her made Harry's heart twang. No matter what the future held for her with Jamie, living closer to Gran wouldn't be the worst decision Harry could make, and leaving her now would be hard to do.

"Off you go, or you'll be late," Gran said.

Harry checked her hair in the hallway mirror one last time and hurried out into the village.

The sun had just dipped down behind the trees that fringed the hillside above the village, and the birds were singing their final goodnights to one another. The evening breeze rippled over Harry's skin, filling her with a sense of easy peace.

"Harry, darling!" A familiar voice rang out from down the quiet street.

Harry didn't need to look to know who'd spotted her. "Mum? This is a surprise," Harry said, forcing a smile.

"I've come to check on your grandmother, and I wanted to see you before you left."

Harry struggled and failed to keep the surprise out of her voice. "I'm just off out to... um... meet some friends."

Harry shifted her shoulders, hoping it would help her relax. Why was it so hard to be herself around her mother? Stupid question. Perhaps it was because Barbara always found something to disapprove of about Harry.

"You and that boy Jamie were quite the hot topic at the wedding last weekend. Sounds like your visit hasn't been all work."

"It hasn't been work at all," Harry said, trying not to sound bitter. "I've enjoyed helping Gran."

"From what I hear, you two have been spending quite a bit of time together."

Harry bit back a comment that yes, she and Gran had been spending lots of time together, but she knew that wasn't what Barbara meant. Her mother had something to say about Jamie, and Harry wished she would just get on and say it without playing all these games first. "What's this about, Mum? What's on your mind?"

Barbara smiled as if she was impressed by Harry's intu-ition. Harry didn't smile back.

"You're a grown woman and it's none of my business, of course."

Harry bit her lip to stop herself from telling Barbara how right she was.

"I just don't want to see you selling yourself short, that's all. You've done so well for yourself, made a life away from here. It's what I always hoped for. I didn't want you to be like me."

Harry took in Barbara's crisp wool slacks and cashmere sweater, the jacket designed with absolute precision to look casual, the imported Italian boots, the casual bounce to her mother's hair, the shades and tones of honey blond that Mother Nature herself had never achieved, and that could only be produced by an expert colorist. "You've done alright for yourself, I'd say. You got away, made a life."

Barbara shook her head so that the evening sun caught her highlights and made them shimmer. For all her faults, her mother was a beautiful woman. "I bought a life," Barbara said. "I bought this hair, this figure, these clothes. I paid for it all in compromise."

"Graham is hardly a compromise," Harry said.

"Smoke and mirrors, darling. Smoke and mirrors."

Harry gripped her lip between her teeth, willing herself to keep her frustration with Barbara at bay. Why must her mother always be so dramatic? But when she noticed the quiver in her mother's lips, the fist throttling Harry's patience relaxed. For the first time in years, perhaps ever, Harry saw the slightest slip of Barbara's mask, a hint that underneath that burnished exterior was an unhappy woman. "Does he... Has he ever hurt you?"

"No. Nothing like that."

"Then what?"

"Everything's a trade-off, that's all I'm saying. And I don't want to see you sacrifice all you've worked for in exchange for a little adoration."

Harry was about to protest, but when she stared at the woman in front of her, she saw her as if for the first time, not as a powerful goddess leaving broken hearts in her wake, but as a soft-centered, damaged woman who'd learned to move through the world in a Teflon coating. But apparently, life didn't bounce off Barbara, after all. Her mother's struggles had found their way through to her soft center.

"I've been happy here, these past few weeks," Harry said. Barbara held her gaze for a moment longer than was comfortable. It felt as if her mother was challenging her, pressing her to look a little deeper. But Harry had been happy. Very happy. "Even with Gran in the hospital, I've enjoyed being here."

"You're on holiday, a vacation. How can you not be happy?"

Harry thought about seeing Gran in the hospital, easing her out of bed each morning, helping her get dressed. "It's not exactly been a vacation," said Harry, laughing.

"But you haven't had to worry about the day-to-day things, have you? It's not the same as living in a place."

"No."

"It's a bit like a summer romance, in a way."

Harry snapped to attention, just in time to catch Barbara's tight expression. So that's where she was going. "You mean Jamie?"

Barbara looked away.

"Mother," Harry said. "If you have something to say, let's hear it. Woman to woman."

"I saw the way he looked at you at the wedding and I saw the way you looked at him. I don't know if it's a summer romance or if it's something else, but that boy is in love with you, Harry."

Harry couldn't argue.

"You broke his heart once, you know that, don't you?" Harry nodded. "And you have the power to break it again.

You always wanted a big life, Harry, even before you were old enough to articulate it, you dreamed big, and I always knew you'd make something of yourself. Be careful you don't throw it all away."

For all the things Barbara had been wrong about, this was the worst. Yes, Harry had done exactly what Barbara had said and built a life in which she called the shots. She'd never had to depend on someone else. She had her own place, her own money, her own life. But, also like Barbara, she had come home a failure. She could tell herself she'd come home only to take care of Gran, but she'd only been able to do that because the rest of her life was in shambles. She'd lost her job, her boyfriend, her dignity, and she'd come home in shame.

But that's where the similarities ended. Because someone always rescued Barbara from her failures, but Harry had options. She could choose to go back to her old life in San Francisco, or she could choose to start a new life in another city, maybe Boston. She could even choose to move back here and live a different life, smaller perhaps, but fuller. The difference was, Harry got to choose.

"Don't worry about me, Mum. I can take care of myself."

She gave Barbara a quick hug and strode off to her date with Jamie.

CHAPTER EIGHTEEN

JAMIE HAD FORGOTTEN to decant the wine. See that, right there, was what Harry did to him. Running a kitchen was a careful blend of creativity and process, and Jamie had always been cool under pressure. Throw Harry into the mix and his brain went off on tangents. He lost track of his details and processes, details like uncorking the wine and giving it time to breathe.

As he dashed to the makeshift staging area to find the decanter, he spotted Harry leaving her gran's. She was early! He took the decanter back to the space his friends had helped him to clear in the restaurant, set it on the table... and breathed. He was nervous, that was all. This was a big night, and he wanted it to be perfect. All he had to do was keep his cool.

He ran over his speech again, making sure he hit all the points Ollie had outlined for him, taking out all the obvious movie quotes. But as he waited for Harry to cross the street and push open the door to what would become his restaurant, he wondered if he'd made a mistake getting relationship advice from Ollie. Ollie had a way with words, no doubt about it, but he was alarmingly short on experience in the romance department. Now Jamie thought about it, he wasn't sure Ollie had ever mentioned a girlfriend, or a boyfriend for that matter. But it was too late now. Harry was on her way.

Jamie cleared his throat and stared at his reflection in the dusty window, thinking through his speech one more time. It had sounded great when they'd rehearsed in the office, Ollie giving stage directions, and coaching Jamie based on his experience as a founding member of the Hope Valley Players. Even Terry, who'd come in to fill out paperwork, had given pointers and deemed his new boss ready to take the plunge.

But now that Jamie was alone with the words, they sounded forced. He took another breath to calm his nerves. He would just be honest with Harry. Forget all his fancy lines. All he had to do was tell her how he felt. How hard could that be?

Tiny prickles like icy footprints ran down Jamie's body. Where was Harry, anyway? She should have been here by now. He rubbed a patch of window clean and peeked out. There was no sign of Harry. Perhaps she'd gone back for something. He checked the time. He'd put the salmon in to time it perfectly, but if Harry was going to be late, he should take it out.

He allowed himself a small smile as he remembered Harry's "salmon en funeral pyre." He'd chosen this dish tonight because it was how they'd been reunited, but now he worried she'd think he was making fun of her.

He peered into the street, and that's when he spotted a familiar blonde head. Harry's mother. And by the looks of it, she'd cornered someone and trapped them in conversation. He hoped it wasn't Harry.

When Harry finally arrived, she looked ashen. "Sorry I'm a bit late," she said. "My mother showed up."

"Everything okay?"

Harry twisted the end of her chin, just the way she always used to when she was worried. "Everything's fine."

The little icy footsteps ran all the way back up Jamie's neck. He'd convinced himself to lay his heart out on the table for Harry to take. He'd taken so many leaps of faith in the past week, and they'd all worked out fine, so far. But now the table felt more like a chopping block, and asking Harry to stay felt like handing her a cleaver.

"Smells delicious," Harry said, sniffing the air. "Is that salmon?"

"It is."

"*En croute?*"

Heat flashed in Jamie's face. "It's my signature dish," he said. He waited for Harry to look offended, but instead she smiled.

"The dish that reunited us," she said, and Jamie finally relaxed.

HARRY SAT at the small wooden table lit by a wreath of garden lights that hung from the ceiling. She nibbled on a bit of the salad that Jamie had set in front of her. Peppery watercress with creamy avocado, and just the tiniest hint of fruitiness. She rolled the flavors around in her mouth, trying to dissect the flavors. All she could say in the end was, "This is amazing."

She could feel Jamie watching her. Finally he gestured to Harry, the table, the room. "*This* is amazing," he said.

Harry took another forkful, chewing carefully so she

could buy time to find the words she needed to say. She thought about her PowerPoint slides, the conversation with her mother. She thought about the wedding, the time she'd spent with Jamie in his kitchen. She thought about this space, Jamie's dream, and the restaurant it would soon become. And she thought about being here to watch this story unfold. She'd been scared for so long, afraid of being like her mother, trapped in someone else's life.

But Harry wasn't her mother. She had to remember that.

"Harry?" Jamie said. He reached across the table and took her hand.

Harry waited. Jamie's mouth twitched as if he were chewing around words to find the perfect ones. She couldn't wait any longer. She pushed up from her seat and walked around the table. He stood to meet her, wrapped her in his arms, and kissed her.

~

JAMIE WRAPPED his arms around Harry and sunk into her beautiful smile. A word made its way to his lips. *Stay*, he wanted to tell her. Stay with me here. Make this dream of mine come true. Be part of it with me. *Stay*.

But what if she said no? What if asking pushed her away? He wanted to keep her here forever, but failing that, he wanted to keep her as long as he could. If he asked and she left, he'd lose her for good.

He leaned closer, kissed her slowly, easily, holding back just a little. And while his lips moved across hers, and her hands pressed into the muscles of his back, he sent a silent message. *Stay with me, Harry Belmont. I still love you.*

HARRY'S LIPS moved across Jamie's, an electric pulse jumping from him to her. I want to stay here forever, she felt herself wanting to say.

For a moment Jamie stopped and pulled away. Harry looked at him and she could read his thoughts. He wanted her. Harry wanted him too. But when she looked at this man and she saw Jamie, she knew she could not break his heart again. She had to be sure.

She was sure.

So when he took her hand and led her from the restaurant, flicking off the oven and abandoning their dinner, she went with him. When he led her through the quiet village to the door of his cottage, she followed. And at the foot of his stairs, her whole body yearning for his touch again, yearning for Jamie Forrest, she made her decision. She led him by the hand up the stairs, and Jamie Forrest followed her to his bed.

CHAPTER NINETEEN

HARRY WOKE up in the pale light of pre-dawn, tangled in the sheets of Jamie's bed. At her back, with his arms wrapped around her, Jamie breathed the sleep of a contented man. Harry lay there for a long time, listening. She felt his abdomen press against her and retreat with each breath, his skin warming hers before the cooler air filled the space left by his exhale. His breathing had the same easy rhythm as the sea in a calm bay, lapping waves up onto the sand and away. Harry closed her eyes and sank into the bliss of an early morning in the arms of a man who stayed.

It was easy to imagine waking up this way every day. But a brief flutter of apprehension passed through her, niggling that it was too soon to make these kinds of plans—she needed to take it slow. She pushed the sensation down and allowed herself the fantasy of a different kind of life. The job that she would apply for in London. Time with Gran as she navigated her golden years. A cozy, loving partnership with Jamie as he followed his passion and dreams. If the past 24 hours were any indication of things to come, it was going to be a beautiful life.

Her stomach growled around the empty spot where Jamie's salmon *en croute* should have been. It was a shame to have wasted it, but well worth the sacrifice. Reluctantly, she pulled away and padded downstairs to make tea and toast.

She'd need to get back to help Gran shower and dress soon. They had lots to talk about, including whether Gran was willing to have a roommate for a while. But for now, Harry still had plenty of time to crawl back into bed with Jamie.

While she waited for the kettle to boil, she turned on the small TV beside the fridge. The morning show hosts sat on a yellow couch discussing the decline in senior care, and how the trend toward smaller families had left many seniors without relatives who, traditionally, would have cared for them. Harry had never thought much about Barbara becoming a senior and needing more help. Her mother and grandmother were both so vibrant and healthy, it was hard to picture them getting old. But Gran's hip had slowed her down more than Harry had imagined, and someday Barbara would slow down too. If Harry got the job in London—and she was more than qualified—she could work mostly from home and be close enough to help Gran. And when the time came, she would be a few hours, rather than a day's travel, away from her mother.

And if she stayed with Gran, she and Jamie could give it another try, find out for certain if they were meant to be together. Home, work, love, all in the same place. Putting down roots instead of always being on the move. It sounded to Harry like a little piece of heaven.

The morning show presenters beamed at the camera and introduced the next segment, a special guest who was here to show everyone how to make the perfect salmon *en croute*. Harry smiled to herself. She bet that this chef's version wouldn't be as good as Jamie's. She should wake him to watch. But he'd looked so peaceful. She'd have to enjoy this alone.

The camera cut to a kitchen island where the male presenter now stood with a stunning woman. She had masses of black curls and a smile that practically glinted under the studio lights. Harry thought she must be a celebrity chef, someone she'd probably seen a million times on the cover of magazines in line at the grocery store. But she couldn't have come up with her name on a bet.

"Alexis," the presenter said, giving the information Harry needed. "You're going to make something very special for us today, I understand."

"This is a very romantic dish, guaranteed to win anyone's heart." She flashed a seductive smile at the camera, and even Harry was pulled in to her charm.

"And this is a dish from your restaurant, is that right?"

"Yes, but it's a special dish, not always on the menu. We make it for Valentine's Day and Mother's Day, sometimes for other special occasions, such as when we know one of our diners is going to propose."

"Sounds like this dish is special to you."

Alexis laughed, flashing her teeth for the viewers. "This was my ex-husband's signature dish. He taught me how to make it and it helped launch my career. I have him to thank for much of my success."

As Alexis explained how to trim the salmon into neat blocks, Harry frowned and spooned coffee into the French press. This Alexis woman was certainly full of herself. As Harry glanced at the screen, a caption flashed up. Harry read it just as the kettle came to a boil. Her eyes darted back to the TV.

ALEXIS MANN, the caption read. FOUNDER OF "SLATE," LONDON.

Harry stared at the TV. Her mind lurched from one thought to another, as if trying to fit together mismatched pieces from a dozen different puzzles. Slate: same name as Jamie's former restaurant. Alexis: same name as Jamie's former wife. Salmon *en croute*: her ex-husband's signature dish. Jamie's signature dish.

"A firecracker," Jamie had said about his ex-wife. "She did great." Harry tried to dig up a memory of the clipping Gran had sent all those years ago. The curls. The smile. This had to be the same woman. "A big wedding," Jamie had said. "Lots of celebrity chefs." His ex-business partner had wanted fame and had found it. Harry watched as Alexis Mann wrapped a neat sheet of pastry around a neat square of salmon. Jamie's ex-business partner. Jamie's ex-wife.

Harry found her clothes where she'd left them the night before. She gathered them together, her mind sifting through all the bits of information she'd just collected. In the bathroom, she fumbled to get dressed, her heart pounding and her throat tightening around a lump of dread.

Jamie had lied to her about Alexis. Only when she'd brought up the topic had he even mentioned he'd been married. And not once in any of their conversations had he mentioned that his former business partner was also his former wife. Now Harry thought about it, there'd been ample opportunity for him to be honest with her, but he always dodged the details. Why so secretive, Jamie? Why not tell the truth? Was he still in love with the woman who broke his heart?

She hurried down the stairs and grabbed her jacket, wrapping it around herself against a cold that came from within. She took a last look at the inside of Jamie's cozy home, where she'd thought she could feel safe, and stepped out into the village.

The first hint of daylight glowed faintly over the distant hills, silhouetting trees and farms, turning up the contrast a notch so that Harry could make out the gate of the cottage across the street, a cat skulking across the empty road. The church clock bonged five chimes into the quiet.

At dawn in San Francisco, the city would be flooded by street lamps and lights from office buildings. The first morning commuters would be wending their way in before the rush, buses and trollies rumbling through the early morning streets; taxis taking people home. Even at dawn, there were people in the streets—those who made the streets their home, runners taking advantage of the quiet, street cleaners, garbage collectors, employees of coffee-houses and 24-hour diners. Even at this hour, the city would be alive. It never really slept.

But the village went to sleep at night. The streets went dark, the trickle of traffic stopped, the lights in the houses went off. Only the glow of the clock on the church tower, watching over the village like a nightwatchman, kept everyone in Hope safe. Harry wouldn't dream of walking the streets of San Francisco alone at dawn, but now she needed to be out in the village's quiet, to be outside in the crisp morning air, and alone with her tangle of thoughts.

What had Jamie told her when he'd first taught her to cook? "You have to focus on what's going on around you." She'd kicked herself about the story she'd created around Tom. And then she'd gone and told herself another story about Jamie. He never talked about his business partner, told her little about his brief marriage, and had neglected to even mention how closely the two were tied. Barbara was right. Harry had been pulled into a vacation romance, only allowing herself to see the sweet side of a life with Jamie. Harry Belmont. Prize Idiot. For the second time in a row.

She had to get practical, get back to her logical self. It wasn't just that Jamie had lied, although she'd had more than her fill of lying men, especially when it came to lies about marriage. He'd shared his dreams with her, and then he'd pulled her into those plans. They both had experience mixing business with pleasure, and they'd both been burned. Jamie seemed perfectly willing to take that risk again. Harry was not.

A set of headlights rounding the corner interrupted her pity party. She lifted a hand to greet the driver she didn't know. No doubt a local farmer on his way to milking. People were friendly here, and strangers greeted one another out of politeness. She felt more a part of this village where few people knew her than she did of the city where she could count hundreds of acquaintances but few real friends. But she couldn't stay. Not now.

She'd been willing to give her relationship with Jamie another chance. Like Nicki said, maybe it was just the wrong time last time. Moving back to Hope, starting a fresh chapter here close to Gran. She could do that. Testing the waters with Jamie, taking a chance on love again. She could do that, too. But smashing Jamie's dreams again... tangling their hearts up with the restaurant... What if it didn't work out between them? What if Jamie had to choose again between the woman he'd once loved and the dream he wanted? He needed to do this on his own this time, follow his dreams his way, without her heart intertwined in it. Maybe in the future, when the restaurant was the success she knew it could be, maybe that would be the time for them to test their feelings. But not now. Harry couldn't risk it.

She wished Gran was awake already. Gran was great at broken hearts. She wouldn't judge, wouldn't say "I told you so", wouldn't warn Harry that she should be more careful about her choice in men. Gran would make Harry a cup of tea, slosh in a shot of whiskey, and listen while Harry told her every little detail of the complete and utter mess she'd made of her life. Again.

At the end of the street Harry stopped. There was a light on in Gran's cottage. She crossed the street, squeaked open the gate, and went around to Gran's back door. As she fumbled with her key, her eyes filled with tears. She blinked them away, promising herself she wouldn't burden Gran with her problems. She swung the door open, kicked off her shoes, and called up to Gran. Jogging up the stairs, she put a brave smile on her face and went to help Gran. As she bent to help her out of bed, Gran wrapped her arms around Harry's neck. Gran smelled warm and sleepy, comfortable and safe. Harry closed her eyes and breathed her in.

"What's all this?" Gran asked, but Harry didn't answer. Without another word, Gran folded her into a warm, Gran-scented hug. Harry clung on until her shoulders relaxed and she folded her head onto Gran's shoulder. And then she let the tears flow.

CHAPTER TWENTY

WHEN JAMIE WOKE UP, his tired body ached, as it often did after a long day on his feet. But this ache was different. This was from a long night with Harry, and it was delicious. He recalled pressing close to her at the restaurant. Pressing even closer at the door to his cottage. Pressing all the way against her in the soft folds of his bed.

He rolled over, stretching his limbs and prying open his bleary eyes. The rumpled sheets beside him were empty. No Harry. A noise drifted in from downstairs. The front door? He listened closer. No, just the TV in the kitchen. Harry was making breakfast? He pictured Harry appearing at the foot of his bed, hair disheveled, long legs sticking out from the bottom of one of his sweatshirts, a mug of steaming coffee in each hand. He smiled at the picture, and every fiber of his weary body tingled back to life.

He pushed up from the bed and slid into a pair of jeans. Padding down the stairs, he rubbed the sleep from his eyes. It was Sunday, blissful Sunday. He and Harry had the whole day ahead of them.

"Morning," he said, ambling into the kitchen. Harry

wasn't there. Steam rose from the spout of the kettle and two mugs were set out on the counter. "Harry?" No answer.

A familiar voice sent the hairs on the back of his neck tingling. It took his sleep-addled brain a moment to recognize the voice and connect it to the image on the screen of the small TV. There, pulling from an oven something that looked an awful lot like his signature salmon *en croute*, was Alexis. A caption blinked on the screen below her. The name of his ex-wife and the name of his ex-restaurant. And Jamie knew that Harry was gone.

HARRY HELPED Gran down the stairs and into the kitchen, settling her in a chair. Then she set about making tea, cutting two door wedges of bread and smearing them with butter and homemade jam. She slid the bread and jam onto a plate and sat down across from Gran.

"Well?" Gran said. "Do you want to talk about it?"

Harry took a bite of the bread, the rich sweetness of the jam tingling her taste buds. She shook her head. "No." Then, "Yes." Then, "No."

Gran waited, watching her, and when she was finally ready, she told her everything. She told her all the sordid details about Tom, how he was the reason she was hunting for a new job. She told her about her plans to move east, and about her creeping desire to put down roots and finally make a home somewhere. And then she told Gran all about Jamie.

"I can't do it, Gran," she said. "What if it doesn't work out?"

"Well, not much in life is guaranteed, Harry. You know

that. You've picked yourself up before and I'm sure you could do it again if you had to."

"But this is different. This is Jamie."

"He's survived a broken heart before."

"I know," Harry said bitterly, thinking about Alexis and the secret Jamie had kept.

"What did he say when you told him you know the truth?"

Harry took a gulp of her tea and looked away. "I didn't wait long enough to find out."

"Oh," Gran said. "Don't you want to know his side of the story?"

Harry pushed the bread and jam away, her appetite gone. "I need more time," she said.

"Then you should take all the time you need, my girl. But I will say this. Don't be afraid to leap just because you can't yet see the net."

A frantic knock at the back door jolted Harry.

"Now, who do you suppose that could be at this hour?" Gran said.

"I don't want to talk to him."

"Harry."

"Will you tell him I'm not here?"

"You don't want to hear what he has to say?"

The knock came again. Harry sighed and went to answer the door. When she glanced back into the kitchen, Gran was hobbling away to the privacy of the living room.

WHEN THE DOOR to Mrs. Belmont's cottage opened, Jamie was both surprised and relieved to see Harry. He'd thought for sure she wouldn't want to talk to him. And he couldn't have blamed her. But here she was. The one that got away. No way was he going to let her get away again. But when he opened his mouth to tell her everything that was in his heart, he was suddenly lost for words.

Harry waited, leaving it to him to explain himself. His heart dropped like an Alka Seltzer in a glass of water and disintegrated in his chest. "Harry," he said, but she held up her hand to stop him.

"I've been doing some thinking," she said.

He bit his lips together.

"Please, Jamie. I need to say this."

He leaned against the door for support and braced himself for what he was now certain would come.

"I have to go home. I've loved being here with Gran. And I've really loved being here with you. But I need to go home and do some thinking away from here."

"Okay. But I have something to say, too." He ran his hand over his cropped hair. Sure he'd now made it stick up, he smoothed it back down again. "We're good together, Harry. We were always good together. And I think if you gave us a chance we could be good together again."

"You said you trusted me. You shared your dreams with me because you trusted me. And so I trusted you. But you lied. Just like Tom, you lied."

Jamie flinched at the name of Harry's ex. The guy was a slimeball, and Jamie had never put himself in that category. But he was there now. "I did lie," he said. "I lied about Alexis because... I don't know... I'm embarrassed. I put all my eggs in one basket—the business, the marriage, all of myself—and then I dropped it. The whole lot. And I came back here a failure. You have no idea how that feels."

"I think I do," Harry said. She smiled. God, he loved that wide, toothy smile. But then it was gone.

"Let's try again, Harry."

She shook her head. "Breaking up with you all those years ago was the hardest decision I've ever had to make. I can't tell you how many times I've thought about you over the years. Wondered what might have happened if we'd stayed together."

"We'd have been amazing."

"Maybe, but if I'd stayed for you, I'd have resented you eventually, always wondering what my life could have been. And maybe you would have resented me, too."

He shook his head. "No way."

"But you have a new dream now, and it's wonderful. And you need to see it through. Your way. Not your ex-wife's way, and not mine."

He couldn't answer that. She was right. He had let Alexis guide his dreams. Was he really making the same mistake again?

"I don't know how the universe works," Harry said. "I don't know why it would put two people together who are clearly good for each other..." Her voice caught. "... and then give them dreams that don't match."

"Maybe it's a test to see what's most important," Jamie said. "What do you choose? Love or dreams?"

Harry didn't answer.

"Or maybe we're not supposed to choose." He could hear the desperation in his voice now. "Maybe we're supposed to figure it out, how to follow the thing we're meant to do and do it with the person we're meant to do it with."

"Maybe you're right."

Jamie perked up. "Well, for me, that person is you. It was always you."

"I'm not the same girl you first fell in love with."

"Are you sure?"

Harry pushed her hair back from her face, that beautiful face that Jamie could look at all day. In that moment he saw the girl he had fallen for, the girl who'd captured his heart. He'd let her go and forgotten to get his heart back before she left. And even though he'd tried to give it to someone else, it had never been there for him to give. He needed his heart back. Even if he got the chance to offer it to Harry again, he needed to reclaim ownership for now.

"I love you," Harry said, and his heart jumped out of reach again. "I think I always have, but I don't see how we can get our paths back together without one of us giving up everything. I don't want to do that and I don't want that for you, either. It was so good—then and now—but it just wasn't meant to be."

Jamie blinked at her. "If you believe that, if you truly believe it, then you need to go home."

But when he looked back at Harry, standing in the doorway of her grandmother's cottage, looked into her eyes that had always been so full of mischief and adventure, he could see that she had already gone.

CHAPTER TWENTY-ONE

AS HARRY'S taxi pulled away at dawn the following morning, she took a last look back at Gran's house. Her grandmother stood in the cottage doorway, fuzzy dressing gown pulled tight and knotted around her small waist. She waved at Harry, a tender smile on her face. Harry waved back. She was going home.

As she turned to face the road ahead, she noticed a light on in Jamie's kitchen. Her neck tensed with the fight between turning for one last glimpse of the man she had once loved—twice loved, really—and the future she knew she must face. She'd made the right decision—for both of them... again. Maybe in some parallel universe they were meant to be together, but here on this planet, they were two shooting stars, whose paths crossed, but were never destined to collide.

The tension in her neck eased as the taxi reached the end of the village. The saying goodbye was done with, and the going home bit was underway. Harry was filled suddenly with a sense of not having stayed long enough, of not doing enough to help Gran, of her stay being fleeting and meaningless, of giving up too quickly on Jamie. Her heart was torn between the desire to go home—to get back to her real life, sleep in her own bed, take the next step in the life she had forged—and the pull to stay. Stay with Gran, stay here in Hope, stay and try one more time to work things out with Jamie.

As the sun eased over the horizon, the cool morning air seemed to wrap around Harry, swaddling her in a comforting glow. Every interaction over the past couple of weeks made her long to be part of the community, made her think of ways she might fit back in. Every view of the area, each tree, every curious cow in the neighboring fields seemed more beautiful as they lured her back into that world. She didn't want to leave, didn't want to say good-bye. But she couldn't stay here any longer.

She glanced behind her through the taxi's rear window, searching for one last glimpse of the village, allowing a hope she was afraid to admit... that Jamie's van would be chasing behind her.

She blinked away the image of the empty road. The thing with Jamie had been a mistake. She needed to accept that. Jamie was familiar, something comfortable and easy at a time when she'd been at her lowest. Falling in love again had been like slipping into a favorite pair of old jeans and an oversized, cozy sweater. They felt good on, fitting in all the right places, allowing room to move with ease. But you couldn't go out in public dressed like that. The outfit was comfortable, but it didn't reflect who you really were.

Jamie was a leftover memory from a happy period of Harry's life. Despite her struggles to deal with Barbara's abandonment, Harry had been content living with Gran back then. Gran had been the most important influence in Harry's life, and she had given Harry the experience of a loving stable home. And Jamie had been part of that. He'd been her first romance, her first experience of a real relationship, that first frizzle of love satiated for the first time. Yes, she had been in love with Jamie back then. The love between *that* Jamie and *that* Harry had been real. But she wasn't that person anymore, and neither was Jamie. She wasn't the person content in a small village; she wasn't the person who'd be happy with the cozy, settled life. Her time with Jamie had rekindled all those old feelings, but it was the old Harry who had relished them. She wasn't that girl anymore. And it was time the new Harry of today went back to her real life.

She turned back to the road ahead, a small, shrinking feeling in her insides. But as the taxi crested the hill and dropped down into the neighboring valley, Harry didn't look back.

FROM HIS KITCHEN WINDOW, Jamie saw Harry's taxi leave. He reached for the keys to his van, knowing if he let her go now, he wouldn't get a second chance at this second chance. He should race to the airport, catch her before she went through security, tell her how he really felt.

But he'd done that already, and she'd left, anyway. He'd let himself fall in love again, and Harry had let him down. What he needed now was to stay focused on his nice, trustworthy work and not let his stupid heart get in the way of things again. Jamie's keys clattered against the counter as he watched the taxi's lights disappear around the bend at the end of the village. He rolled up his sleeves, washed his hands and went to cook Harry Belmont out of his mind.

He peered at the scrawled notes for a new dish for

Home. The idea had come in the middle of the night, when he'd finally given up on sleep and scribbled it down. Now, as he minced shallots for the sauce, he tried to lift his mood. He was free now to focus on what he truly loved. Local Goodness would flourish with his new staff, and Home would be everything he'd dreamed of now that he could give it his full attention. He allowed himself a vision of his opening night. Friends and family gathered in the cozy light of the bistro. Rich aromas drifting from the kitchen. Laughter, wine, smiling faces. A speech. He'd make a short, witty speech thanking everyone for their support. He'd raise a glass to everyone and throw his arm around the woman who'd inspired him to go for his dreams.

But Harry wouldn't be there.

The daydream exploded like a bag of dropped flour, all his joyful fantasies floating in a cloud to the floor.

Maybe Michael was right. Jamie had allowed Harry Belmont under his skin again, allowed her to fuel him with *her* dreams for his future.

"Is this restaurant your dream or Harry's?" Michael had asked him.

Jamie had sworn the dream was his own.

"Is your dream the restaurant or is it Harry Belmont?" Michael had asked next.

It had been both. But they had come as a package in his mind. But now they were separated, he wasn't sure he had it in him to see the restaurant through. Local Goodness was already a success. Surely that was enough?

Stupid, stupid, idiotic man, Jamie thought. He'd mixed business and pleasure again, and now he couldn't pull the two apart. Well, he'd show her. He'd show Harry Belmont he didn't need her inspiration to follow his dreams. He'd learned the hard way who he could trust, and that person was himself. From now on, this would be Jamie's show.

He scraped the shallot into a bowl, scribbled another note in his book, and focused on his work, the thing he truly loved. There was only one time that he pictured Harry's face. And that was every time he blinked.

CHAPTER TWENTY-TWO

HARRY DUMPED her suitcase inside the door of her apartment and took in the familiar sights. A pile of mail, mostly junk, teetered on the small table. The galley kitchen was clean, probably unused, and more-or-less as Harry had left it. Taz's sister had left a bottle of wine and a note for Harry, telling her how much she'd enjoyed her stay, and how lucky Harry was to live in this beautiful city. None of it made her feel she was home.

But there was Spike, sitting on the windowsill. She hurried over to check on him. He was alive and well.

"Spike! I'm home!" Harry said, but the little cactus didn't respond. Taz was already at work and, apart from the hum of the refrigerator, the apartment was absolutely silent. No laughter, no aromas of cooking, no one to talk to except Spike.

Harry swallowed hard and blinked at the city from her tall windows. Life bustled between the towering buildings, the green squares of parks in between, a slash of water in the distance where the city met the bay, the arch of a bridge linking one mass of land to another. She'd loved the city's diversity, how people from all corners of the world had found their way here as the city grew. The owner of Giovanni's, her favorite Italian restaurant, was the third generation to run it. She lived among elderly Chinese and young Indians, people of all ages from every corner of the globe. Anyone could belong in San Francisco and come to call it home. But it was time for Harry to move on. She took a shower and went down to Giovanni's to eat.

"Bella Harrietta," Giovanni called in his fake Italian accent when he saw her. "You come back, eh?"

"For now," Harry said.

He dropped the gusto—and the accent—and got serious. "How was home? How's your grandma doin'?"

"Better than ever," Harry said.

"I thought maybe you'd stay, you know? Maybe settle down, have a couple of kids, get out of the rat race." He elbowed Harry in a friendly dig.

Harry smiled, not able to manage a laugh. "Not me, Giovanni. You knew I'd be back."

But Giovanni shook his head. "Come on, Harry. This isn't where we belong. This city is a great place to live, make a big success of yourself, have nice things. But this isn't home, not for people like you and me."

Harry considered Giovanni. They talked like this whenever she came in. Giovanni always waxing about "the old country", talking of home and family, Harry telling stories about Gran. "But you were born here," Harry said, laughing. "This is home for you."

Giovanni shook his head. "My youngest graduates college next year, God willing. My kids don't want to run a restaurant. My wife and me, we've done our job. My brother's kid is going to take over. Smart lady she is. We're gonna move to Genoa, back to our roots. I was born here, sure, lived my whole life here, but my heart..." He put a meaty hand to his chest. "My heart's always been in Italy."

Harry had a fleeting thought about Giovanni's closed-up restaurant, allowed herself a brief daydream of Jamie opening up his restaurant in its place. Jamie's concept would do really well here. But Jamie wouldn't. Not away from the place he loved most, the friends like Michael he'd known since childhood. Jamie loved the quiet of the village and the rolling hills stretching to the horizon. From her table at Giovanni's, all she could see was concrete and noise. A cable car clanged by, a truck honked its air horn, her view was obscured by a new wave of people hurrying by. Jamie would hate it here. They were different people, she and Jamie. She shook her head and forced the thought of him away.

"You look sad," Giovanni said.

"Not sad, just thinking."

"Home is where you're happiest, Harry. Don't forget that."

Harry didn't have much time to think more about Giovanni's retirement plans or what Jamie would be doing now. The following morning, she was up at dawn, sorting out her life and making plans to move to Boston. She ordered boxes from the moving company, put in calls about three apartments within walking distance of her new office, and promised Taz to help her find a new roommate. All she had to do now was accept the job offer, but that could wait until Friday. She didn't want to appear desperate.

In the afternoon, she went to her old office and signed an affidavit documenting her relationship with Tom. Harry had been strangely reluctant when Judith had asked, but once she'd agreed, she knew it was just her foolish pride holding on to some hopeless idea that Tom hadn't really betrayed her. Just like Jamie hadn't betrayed her with his lies.

When she was done with the statement, she was tempted to sign it Harry Belmont, Prize Idiot, and add a postscript. P.S. I will never, ever, ever mix business and pleasure again.

As she handed over the document, Harry steeled herself for Judith's mocking tone, waited to hear the patronizing sneer in her voice. But Judith surprised her.

"He really is a piece of work," she said. "Just a smooth operator. I'm only sorry we didn't spot this behavior sooner and prevent the damage he caused."

No mocking. No tone that suggested Judith would never have been so gullible. She seemed to carry genuine responsibility that a predator like Tom Steele had slipped through her hawk-like hiring process.

"Your position is still open," Judith said. "We'd love to have you back."

A brief feeling of triumph coursed through Harry, but it fizzled out fast. Even if she thought it was a good idea to return to the company that had been so hasty to cut her loose, accepting the offer would be going backward, and Harry always kept moving forward. But it was more than that. Staying in San Francisco would be an awful lot like putting down roots, and that was a dangerous thing. "Thanks," she said, shaking her head. "But it's time for me to move on."

Harry arrived home to find a large stack of moving boxes and a small stack of delivered boxes outside her door.

Her meal kits had arrived. As she slid the heavy boxes inside with her foot, she thought about Jamie's caring service, how he'd carried in his meal kit boxes and set them on Gran's kitchen table. How Gran had chatted his ear off as he'd unpacked them for her. How he'd stayed that first evening and cooked salmon *en croute*. Harry's stomach shriveled. Salmon *en croute*, his signature dish, the one he'd used to woo Alexis, the one that had almost trapped her, too.

In the tiny kitchen, Harry slipped Thai chicken and vegetables with brown rice into the microwave and set it to heat as she put the remaining meals away. Two in the fridge for the next two nights and the rest in the freezer for next week. She took a shower, put on her PJs and, when the timer went off, carried her dinner to the table. It was only Tuesday, not a day she normally drank when she was working, but she opened the bottle from Taz's sister and poured herself a glass.

She'd ordered this particular meal several times. It was one of her favorites, but tonight it tasted bland, just fuel to put in her body to carry her through to the next day. Perhaps she should make an effort to cook sometimes. Jamie had given her that confidence. When she was settled in Boston, she should look for a meal kit service like Local Goodness, one that sourced ingredients from local farmers. Spending forty-five minutes to create something tasty and home-cooked would be good for her health, and it would be a nice way to unwind at the end of the day.

She clicked on her phone, intending to do a spot of research while she ate. There was an email from her new boss-to-be, asking if she'd made a decision and if she could start a week earlier. They'd pay for any additional moving costs, plus temporary accommodation, because a new project had come up with a tight deadline and they'd love for Harry to dive right in.

Harry knew from experience that "a tight deadline" would mean long hours and weekends. Who was she kidding, that she could come home each night and cook a leisurely dinner for herself? By the end of her first week, she'd be lucky to have the energy to heat one of her prepared meals. Giovanni was right, big cities were where you went to be a success, have nice things. Her apartment with a view of the city hadn't come from working nine-to-five hours and cooking meals in her spare time. That was what you did when you were ready to settle down.

Harry's mind flashed to Jamie and the afternoons they'd spent cooking together, eating and talking at his table. And she thought about the meals she'd shared in Gran's company. In the silence of her apartment, she scraped the last of the rice into her composting bin, rinsed the plastic tray for recycling, and took the bottle of wine to bed.

Despite still recovering from the fatigue of travel, Harry lay there for hours, watching the lights of the city move across the ceiling. She'd climbed into this bed alone on so many nights. She'd liked sleeping alone, liked the sprawl of the bed, sleeping and getting up on her own schedule, reading until late without disturbing someone else. But tonight she wasn't just going to bed alone, she was going to bed lonely. It was that difference that kept her awake.

Harry had four moving boxes packed the next morning when Gran called. The sound of her grandmother's voice made something catch in Harry's chest.

"I miss you already," she told Gran.

"Jamie popped in earlier," Gran said.

"Oh?" Harry said, trying to sound calm. "What did he want?"

"Just a chat."

"Oh. About me?"

"Not really."

"Oh."

"That boy's in love. You know that, don't you?"

Harry said nothing. She knew.

"And are you?"

"No," she said quickly. *Am I?* Harry thought. *Am I in love with Jamie Forrest?* "I don't think so," she added.

"Oh, Harry," said Gran.

"Oh, Gran," said Harry. "What am I going to do?"

"What do you want to do?"

Harry didn't have an answer. She didn't seem to have any answers anymore. She'd let herself fall into Jamie and savor what it felt like to be truly loved. She'd wanted to spend more nights with him, waking up in his arms. And she'd wanted to spend days with him, taking the time to get to know him all over again. She wanted to help him open his restaurant, help him put together a business plan, be there when he opened the doors to his first customers. She wanted to circulate and chat with their guests while Jamie worked the room, taking kudos and reveling in his newfound success.

And when everyone left, and they closed up for the night, she wanted to go home with Jamie, to pour him a glass of wine, and sink into the big comfy armchair with him. She wanted to send him for a shower to wash away the day's hard work, and to be waiting in bed for him when he was done. She wanted to be with Jamie. Not just for a night, not even for a few nights. She wanted to be with him forever.

But forever wasn't possible.

"I want to get on with my life," Harry said.

"So, it was just a fling?"

"No!"

"Okay, not a fling. A rebound?"

Harry laughed, oddly uncomfortable giving intimate details of her love life to her grandmother, and yet grateful for Gran's pragmatic approach. "Not a rebound," she said, and she knew that was true. You have to bound before you can rebound, and the thing with Tom had never been real.

"A comfort shag, then?"

"Gran!"

"I'm just trying to help you get to the bottom of this. He's familiar, comfortable, a little nostalgia perhaps?"

Harry shook her head. "He was familiar, and he was comfortable. But it was new, too. Different. Nice."

"So, then," Gran said. "Sounds to me like maybe this is something else entirely. Maybe the real thing?"

Harry closed her eyes, blotting out the truth Gran had spoken. But the images that danced across the insides of her eyelids were all of Jamie. Jamie in a smart lemon-colored shirt, leading her onto the dance floor. Jamie in his kitchen teaching her to cook. Jamie helping Gran into her chair, patiently moving at Gran's slow pace. And Jamie in his bed. Jamie in her arms. Jamie with her.

"Oh, Gran," Harry said. "What am I going to do?"

"I'm not sure, my girl," Gran said. "But it sounds to me like you've gone and fallen in love."

"But it can't work, can it? He's there. I have a life here. I have..." But Harry couldn't finish the sentence. *I have what?*

She had an apartment and friends, a career. She had a life that was worlds away from Jamie's. But as she sat on the phone with Gran, she wondered how much of that she could walk away from.

"I can't come home," she said.

"You're not your mother," Gran said.

Harry's breath caught.

"There's a difference between coming home because you want to and coming home because you *have* to. I can't say I wouldn't enjoy having you around more, but it's your life, not mine. It would be a big change for you, a different lifestyle. There'd be things you'd lose and things you'd gain, whatever you choose to do. Everything is a compromise, Harry. You just have to decide for yourself what's important to you, what kind of life you want to live."

"My mother warned me not to put roots down there. She said I'd end up stuck."

"Tosh. What your mother never understood is that you can't spread your branches wide if you don't have firm roots. Any tree will tell you that."

Harry had never wanted to put down roots, but as she looked at the moving boxes piling up in her apartment, she wondered how it would feel to settle down.

That night, Tom called. Harry looked at his name on her screen, her thumb hovering over the Dismiss Call button. He shouldn't be calling her in the middle of his investigation. No doubt he was trying to weasel his way in to get her to drop her story. But still, her thumb slid over and landed on the green Answer.

"Harry." His voice was warm and liquid, like strong hot coffee on a cold, foggy morning. "I heard you were home. How was England? How's your grandmother doing?"

"What do you want, Tom?"

"I want you, Harry. I've always wanted you."

She was tempted to throw her phone against the kitchen wall, watch it shatter into tiny fragments, imagining Tom's lies exploding with it, disintegrating into a million pieces on her kitchen floor.

"I know, Tom," she said. "I know you always wanted me."

"Harry..."

"But you also wanted Meredith and who knows how many other women."

"It was only ever you, Harry."

"And was it only Meredith when you told her that at the altar?"

"We've separated. I'm moving out, getting my own place in the city, somewhere you and I can be together instead of hiding."

"What changed?"

"We outgrew one another. You know how it can be."

"I do know. I've outgrown you, Tom. I need a grownup, a man who respects me, someone I can be with, not hide away. I want someone to build a life with and a home and maybe even a family. I want someone who loves me, Tom. And that someone isn't you."

She hung up the phone and closed her eyes, Tom's face lingering behind her eyelids. She squeezed them tighter, squashing him out, and when the sparkly lights cleared she saw her gran, alone in her cottage. She saw the faces at the wedding, all the people who had pulled her so warmly into their circle. She saw Jamie's cozy living room, his kitchen table strewn with ingredients.

And then she saw Jamie. Jamie checking all the boxes on the list of the things Tom wasn't, everything about him feeling so right.

She looked out over the city and wondered if she had it all wrong. Everything about Jamie felt so permanent, so rooted and unmoving. She'd always seen that as a bad thing, fine for others, but not for her. But everything here felt temporary. Tom fleeting, her new job in Boston unknown.

Giovanni spending his whole life here, but always waiting for the chance to go home.

Harry sank to her stiff occasional chair. She'd made the biggest mistake of her life and now she was 6,000 miles too far away to undo it.

CHAPTER TWENTY-THREE

"LOVELY DAY FOR IT," said Terry as Jamie peered through the water gushing across the van's windshield. It had rained non-stop since Harry left. The sky varied from slate gray to pale gray, allowing flecks of teasing blue to peek through once in a while. It seemed to Jamie that the rain was heaviest in the brief spells between him and Terry getting out of the van to make a delivery, and getting back in to drive to their next stop. In between, he was sure the rain eased off, tormenting him just because it could. He wondered if the universe was sending him a sign that he was right to hand the Local Goodness operations off to Terry, or if was just providing an appropriate backdrop for Jamie's underlying mood.

He had three restaurant staff candidates coming in to interview later that day. He'd kept putting off scheduling the appointments until Ollie pointed out that, if he didn't move soon, he might lose the chance. Then the building contractor had called to say a job had cancelled, and they were ready to start the demo three weeks earlier than planned. Jamie could have interpreted this as a sign he'd made the right decision, too. But it didn't feel that way. He wouldn't say he had cold feet, but if he'd put them on his boxes of food, there'd be no need for the expensive refrigeration system in his van.

As the van crunched up the driveway of Hilltop Farm, the rain stopped. Jamie couldn't find a way to turn that into either a good or bad omen for his plans. Before he'd even unloaded the boxes, Callum and Jess's beagles pushed around the door and sprinted to him. Jamie bent to greet them. But at the last second, they wheeled past him and gathered around Terry's legs. Surely that was a sign that hiring Terry was the right move, and yet Jamie couldn't help feeling he'd been so quickly forgotten.

He pulled himself together and introduced Terry, explaining to Callum about the new roles they'd each be playing as Home became a reality.

"The girls are fickle," said Callum. "They'll fawn over anyone. But Jess and I will miss seeing you."

"You can always come down to the restaurant," Jamie said.

"Of course," Callum said. "Sure."

Jamie scratched the dogs' heads, being sure to give equal time to each set of jealous ears. He wasn't sure when he'd see them again. "We'd better be off then," he said at last. "Hope to see you soon."

Callum shook his hand. "Thanks for all the great food. And the excellent company. I know you're going to make a success of it."

Jamie nodded, an uncharacteristic lump forming in his throat. He tried to tell Callum that he wouldn't be far away, but it felt more like he was saying goodbye forever, and the words wouldn't come.

When they drove back into the village, Jamie pulled

over to the side of the road and parked across from the empty shop that would soon become his dream restaurant. He stared at the shuttered building through the rain that had started up again, trying to see again the possibilities that Harry had seen. That day he had been able to visualize all that she saw, all the potential, but now when he looked at it, all he saw was a shabby old building in a gray rainy village. All he saw was another failed restaurant that no one was ever going to come to.

"The place is a dump, isn't it?" Jamie said.

"It is," said Terry. "But it's your dump."

"If that was supposed to make me feel better, you failed."

Terry laughed. "Ever heard of Isaac Newton?"

"The apple guy."

"That's the one. Clever bloke, he was. He had these laws of motion."

Jamie frowned. "Can't say science was my favorite subject. I was more of your artsy type."

"I'll forgive you," Terry said. "Anyway, Newton, he had these three laws. He said that a body at rest will stay at rest unless some outside force acts on it. So like, a snooker ball won't move unless a cue or another ball hits it."

"Makes sense."

"He also said that the rate of change of momentum is directly proportional the force applied."

"I'm sorry, Terry, but you're losing me. What's this got to do with the dump across the street that I've just committed to?"

"I'm getting to it. Newton's third law says that when two objects interact, they apply equal forces to one another. So here's the point I'm getting to." He stuck one finger up in the air. "That woman, what's her name?"

"Harry?"

"Yeah, Harry. Harry waltzes in, finds you sitting around —a body at rest—and prods you into action with this restaurant. First law."

"I wasn't exactly sitting around, but okay."

Terry extended a second finger. "Second law, she's here, applying force to you, because you've gone and fallen hard for her, as far as I can see. You're speeding along making plans, and then she leaves. No outside force. Suddenly you start doubting yourself."

Jamie shrugged. "I suppose."

"No suppose about it. I'm watching it. One minute you're going to open your dream restaurant, the next you've got a face like a wet Monday and your dream is just a dump."

Jamie squirmed in his seat. He probably ought to fire Terry for insubordination or something, but he was hitting just a little too close to the truth.

"Law three," Terry said.

"Two objects interacting, right?"

"Right. So you *are* paying attention. Good. The point I'm getting to is that you think she applied this force to you, got you moving, then went home like nothing happened."

"That sounds about right," Jamie said, starting to grow a little impatient and wishing Terry would get to the point.

"But that's not how physics works. She applied a force to you, yes, but you applied an equal and opposite force to her."

"What are you saying?"

"I'm saying that if you think she's gone back to her life completely unaffected by you, you're wrong, my friend."

"Well, that's fine," said Jamie, "but she made it pretty clear we're done."

Terry shrugged. "You can't know that for yourself unless you see where she's ended up."

"Where she's ended up is on the other side of the world, Terry. As in, not here."

"Physically, yes. But mentally?"

"I don't think I know what you're saying, Terry. Sorry, mate."

"I'm saying it's none of my business, but if I were you, I wouldn't just trust that she's over you. I'd go and see for myself."

TWO DAYS LATER, Jamie Forrest was halfway across the Atlantic when he realized he still had no idea what Terry was talking about. But it was too late to turn back now. He had to trust that this new, crazy idea would work out. One way or another, he was about to find out.

CHAPTER TWENTY-FOUR

ON THURSDAY EVENING, Harry stepped out of the elevator across from her apartment door and wondered if she could make the dozen or so steps or if she should just curl up and go to sleep right there in the middle of the floor. She'd been home for three days now, and she could no longer blame her tiredness on jet lag. At Gran's she'd been busy, on the go all day, collapsing into bed each night with fatigue. But it was the kind of physical fatigue that led to deep, peaceful sleep. What Harry felt now was weariness. She had to make her final decision about Boston tonight and call in the morning. She'd been going through the motions of planning her cross-country move. She'd grabbed lunch on the go, cramming in bites between appointments and phone calls, and kept herself busy.

But even as she kept moving forward, some lingering doubt pulled her back. One minute she convinced herself that going back to Hope would allow her and Jamie to get to know one another better as the adults they now were; the next she imagined the mess she would make if she had it wrong and it didn't work out. What if Gran was right, that it was just a summer romance? What if Barbara was right, that she would always regret going home? She couldn't put herself—or Jamie—through another break-up. The path of least resistance was to stay here and put Jamie Forrest behind her once and for all. But the constant push and pull was exhausting.

She propelled her weary body towards the door, but before her key reached the lock, the hair on her neck bristled and she froze. The dulled sounded of laughter came from behind the door. A familiar timbre to the man's voice. Maybe Taz was interviewing potential new roommates, or even had a friend over. But Harry's intuition prickled with the feeling that something was off.

Tom. It was Tom's voice. He'd charmed his way into her apartment. That weasel. She reached for the door again, determined to confront Tom and tell him that, no matter how available he now claimed to be, and no matter how desperate and lonely she was, she would never in a million years go back to him.

"Here she is," Taz called, meeting Harry at the door.

"Taz," Harry whispered. "I don't want to talk to him."

"But he came all this way, and he seems so sweet."

Harry's heart sank. "That's how he operates, Taz. I thought you were wilier than that."

"I just thought..." Taz said.

Harry sighed, steeling herself to face Tom. But something in the air caught her attention. There was the undeniable smell of sauteed garlic and fresh herbs, and the rich scent of something meaty that had been cooking slowly for a long time.

Harry's heart sank. "And he's making dinner. Great."

Harry pushed past Taz and marched into the kitchen. The small dining table had been set for two, with several sets of silverware beside each of Harry's blue plates. In the middle, the wine bottle that Harry had emptied the previous night stood with a candle burning, its flame flickering in the dim evening light. Taz glanced at Harry and raised her eyebrows in approval. Harry shook her head. This was just like Tom to turn on the full strength of his charm, but she was done falling for it.

Just then, he stepped from the kitchen.

"Welcome home," said Jamie.

It took Harry a second to erase her anger at Tom and replace it with confusion at seeing Jamie. "What are you doing here?"

"Let me pour you a glass of wine and I'll tell you everything."

Jamie invited Taz to stay for dinner, but she only laughed. "You are a true gentleman to offer, but I have a feeling that you two need to spend some time alone." She winked at Harry. "Try not to keep me awake too late."

Harry took the glass of wine from Jamie and followed him into the kitchen. A saucepan and her frying pan stood on the stove, steam rising from below the lids. Something delicious was roasting in the oven.

Jamie reached up into Harry's cabinet to take down a pan from the rack and she caught a flash of smooth skin beneath his shirt.

"What are you doing here?" Harry asked.

"Cooking dinner for you."

"You know what I mean. What are you doing here, halfway around the world?"

He gave her an awkward smile. "Not on an empty stomach. It's almost ready." He set two plates on the counter. "Fresh Dungeness crab cakes and local arugula salad to start. And of course, Sonoma County wine."

"It looks wonderful," she said.

"So do you."

Harry's face heated. She tried to ignore it. "I'm glad you're here. It's really nice to see you. Weird, but nice. But you have to tell me what's going on."

Jamie laughed, the way he always did when he was trying to calm his nerves. It was so endearing and she could see the boy she'd first fallen in love with. "I've been thinking about dreams," he said. "You were always such a big dreamer, and I loved that about you. You helped me see a bigger future than I could ever have imagined for myself. You acted on your dreams. I didn't always love that about you, but I respected it. All those years ago, I knew I had to let you go. I told myself if it was meant to be, you'd come back for me. And you did." He laughed again. "Eventually."

Harry started to defend herself, to tell him that she did what she needed to do, but Jamie held up his hand. "Let me finish. The thing is, Harry, you inspired me to follow my dreams, even back then. But I got it all wrong. The restaurant with Alexis, that was never me. It was always what I thought I was supposed to do to be successful. You encouraged me to have my own restaurant, and Alexis made it all look possible. But I never stopped to think about what I wanted."

"And what was that?"

He shrugged. "That's the problem. I didn't know. You broke my heart, Harry Belmont." He smiled. "But Alexis broke my trust. Not just in others but in myself."

He stirred the sauce, focusing as if collecting his thoughts. Harry waited, not daring to interrupt.

"And then you can back," he said. "And I found the restaurant space, and finally I had a vision of what I really wanted. And there you were, all tangled up in it. And I couldn't separate what I felt about you from my excitement about the restaurant. And when you found out about Alexis, I should have fought for you. But I didn't trust myself that I had it right. So I let you go." He frowned at Harry. "Not my best move."

He abandoned the plates and moved towards Harry. "I want to give us a second chance, Harry. Come home with me."

Harry looked at the lights of San Francisco, her stark apartment, and the man at her table. She was tired of being lonely. She was tired of always being on the move. She was tired of trying so hard not to become her mother that she had never been able to become herself.

She took the wooden spoon from Jamie and stirred languidly, trying to settle her thoughts. The spoon left a dark pathway in the pan, and the rich, creamy sauce oozed slowly to fill it. She took a gulp of wine, trying to quench the smoldering fire that Jamie Forrest had lit. And then she knew.

She turned off the stove. "I have another idea," she said. She took Jamie's hand and led him to her bedroom. Giovanni was right that home is where you're happiest. Sometimes it was the place you were from, and sometimes it was the place your heart lived. Sometimes home had nothing at all to do with geography. And there, in her sparse apartment in a big city, wrapped in the comfort of Jamie's arms, everything familiar, everything just as it should be, Harry Belmont was finally home.

Six Months Later

THE SMELLS COMING from the kitchen ignited Harry's tastebuds like a Bonfire Night fireworks display. There was a nutty smell of sesame and peanut, and a tang of fresh cilantro and crispy vegetables. Her stomach growled as she peered through the doorway to where Jamie stood at the stove. He tossed a wok, flipping splashes of color into the air. Bright red chilies, green coriander, flashes of crisp vegetables, and golden creamy peanut sauce. Harry's mouth watered.

"Pad Thai," Jamie said. "Want to taste it?"

Before Harry could answer, Jamie swirled a mouthful of noodles on a set of chopsticks, snatched up a succulent pink shrimp, dipped it in a dab of peanut sauce and presented it at Harry's lips. She opened her mouth and felt the warm flavors on her tongue, the tender noodles, the firmness of the shrimp, the crunch of fresh veggies, and the rich silky smoothness of the peanut sauce. She closed her eyes and let the flavors fill her mouth. Her body warmed, and the tension of her busy workday eased away. She wondered if she could stay like this forever.

"Is it okay?" Jamie asked.

All Harry could do was nod. She didn't want to lose this sensation and if she spoke, she feared the moment would go away and never come back.

"What does it need?" Jamie said.

"Another bite?"

He delivered and took a taste for himself. She watched him taste, his expert palette picking apart the flavors and assessing their impact.

Harry tasted and tried to gauge, too. She wasn't a cook—she'd demonstrated that—but as she'd helped Jamie with his new recipes, she had slowly learned to analyze flavors and know what a dish needed, rather than only knowing whether it was good or not. She took a moment to taste. The kick from the chili was right, just enough to let her know the little firebombs were there, but not enough to blast the rest of the flavors. The saltiness was perfect, bringing out the flavors of the shrimp. She pressed the last bit against the roof of her mouth. There was a... something... a what... a heaviness?

"It needs a lift," Jamie said.

Harry took another taste of the dish. He was right.

"More lime." He squeezed half a lime over the pan and stirred it in. "Try this."

Harry tasted again. The heaviness was gone. In its place was a freshness, a feeling of eating the dish with a cool breeze blowing. "It's perfect."

Jamie beamed at her and scribbled a note on his pad.

"Are you ready?" Harry asked.

Jamie's face twisted into a skeptical expression. "I don't know."

Harry moved closer and wrapped her arms around his waist. "You're ready," she said. She leaned up and kissed Jamie, the heat from the chilis doused by the heat from his lips.

"Can we just stay here forever?" Jamie said.

"Forever?" Harry asked.

"Yes, please."

Harry smiled and kissed him again. It was a familiar kiss, one she'd known for as long as she could remember. She'd let that kiss go once, and like a prize idiot, she'd let it go again. But now that she had a third chance at that kiss, she would never let it get away from her again.

"We can stay here as long as you like," she said. "But first we have some people to feed."

AS JAMIE PLATED the last dishes and slid them across the counter for his new server, he allowed himself to savor a brief a moment of quiet in the kitchen... *his* kitchen. From the dining area, he could hear the ebb and flow of voices and the tinkle of knives and forks against plates. It was a beautiful sound. He moved to the doorway and looked out over the floor of Home. His parents sat a table for two in the window nook. Michael and Sarah were with Harry's gran at a four-top. Sarah's hand drifted to her belly, and Jamie wondered how much longer they were going to wait to announce their news. Nicki drifted between the tables, always the hostess, even when the guests weren't hers. She chatted to Ollie, rested a hand on Terry's broad shoulder, and lingered for some time with Cameron McKenzie. As she moved off to greet someone else she knew, she turned and caught Jamie's eye. She winked, and Jamie felt his face unfold into an enormous smile.

"It's time," said a voice beside him. His favorite voice of all. Harry took his hand and led him to the center of the room. "If I can have your attention," she called, but few of the excited guests heard her. Nicki clanged on a glass with a knife, and a few more people settled. Then Terry stood and yelled, "Quiet, please!" The room fell silent.

Jamie looked around at the sea of expectant faces, his first full capacity night. He beamed at Harry and threw his arm around her, pulling her close beside him. Her body fit tight against his, just where it had always belonged. He leaned in and brushed his lips against her hair, taking in her beautiful, warm scent. And then he threw out his arm and grinned at the crowd. "Dearly beloved," he said, and everyone laughed. "It's my great, great pleasure to welcome all of you Home."

HARRIET "HARRY" Belmont was halfway home when she realized her remarkable life was, in fact, absolutely perfect. She slipped her hand into Jamie's as they walked through the late-night quiet of the village.

"Let's go home," she said.

STAY IN TOUCH

From time to time, I send Maggie Wild Love Letters with details on upcoming new releases, special offers, and other goodies relating to the Hope Valley Romance series. You can stay in touch by signing up at: MaggieWild.com.

Enjoy this book? Share the love

Reviews are a powerful way to share books you love with other readers. And for authors, they're like little virtual hugs.

If you enjoyed this book, I would gratefully accept a hug (even a tiny one-sentence hug) in the form of a review of Amazon, Goodreads, or wherever you talk about books online.

Many thanks and big hugs back,
Maggie

ALSO BY MAGGIE WILD

She needs someone she can count on. He's gun-shy after being hurt. Can a brush with fate in a rained-out English village turn into enduring love?

Sarah Tildon thinks she's found the perfect man. But after her overbearing future mother-in-law insists her quiet country wedding become a high-society shindig, she sets out on a two-week ride to rethink her plans. Stranded when her bicycle is stolen in a picturesque hamlet, she's touched by the kindness of a handsome young farmer who comes to her rescue.

The big city failed Michael Marsden's ample ambitions. After his fiancée cheats on him, he turns his back on the hustle and bustle and takes on a farm to prove he can lead a self-sufficient life. And taken by surprise when a charming outsider helps sing his hens into laying, he realizes his newfound Eden is missing its Eve.

Unexpectedly falling for the sweet homesteader, Sarah is torn between the security of a gilded cage and the precarious freedom of raising chickens. And when her fiancé arrives to bring her back to London, Michael fears she'll leave him with yet another shattered heart.

Will this unlikely couple throw caution to the wind and embrace a destined second chance?

Simply You is the first book in the heartwarming Hope Valley Romance series. If you like fun heroines, pastoral backdrops, and endearing courtships, then you'll adore Maggie Wild's sweet tale.

Buy Simply You to start fresh today!

ACKNOWLEDGMENTS

I wrote the messy first draft of this book on a train, on a boat, and in my childhood bedroom. But to turn it into a book, I had lots of help.

I am grateful to the Uninventables for the morning writing sessions that kept me going. The Inessential Workers offered support and encouragement when things got tricky. Big thanks to my first readers, Kathleen Guthrie Woods and Rosa Kwon Easton for the honest and encouraging feedback. My gratitude to Laurie Johnson for the tough love editing that made this book so much better. Eddy Bay's sharp eye for detail saved me from embarrassing myself.

Finally big hugs and much love to Mum for providing the inspiration for Harry's story. And J for being my Jamie. It was always meant to be you.

ABOUT MAGGIE

Maggie Wild lives in California Wine Country with her own Mr. Right and a small collection of furry friends. A native of Yorkshire, England, she visits "home" every day through her fictional worlds. When not writing her fun, contemporary romance stories, she loves to watch the birds in her garden and hike through the local redwoods.

Learn more at MaggieWild.com.

@maggiewildbooks

www.ingramcontent.com/pod-product-compliance
Lightning Source LLC
Chambersburg PA
CBHW021656110726
47902CB00007B/1955